THE WEDDING WINGER

THE ZAMBONI DIARIES
BOOK 1

DELANCEY STEWART

PROLOGUE

JULIUS RAMON (AKA ZAMBONI DRIVER)

In my experience, there are three things that can really get pro hockey players riled up:

1. Getting checked from behind,
2. Anyone touching your goalie — even the most accidental brush can get a whole bench on the ice with fire in their blood, and . . .
3. Falling in love.

Hockey players are a special breed. They're fiercely loyal, utterly fearless, and at least a little bit unhinged. You have to be, to voluntarily participate in a sport where the odds of being injured are better than fifty percent per thousand hours of play.

The truth?

These guys don't care. They don't worry about the future, they don't internalize the risk. They're in it for today, for now. They play for their brothers on the ice, and they protect and defend them like family. Because they are family.

And when a woman edges her way into one of those fiery hearts?

Anything can happen.

But if the woman is worth the risk, and if she can take the heat, then the hockey player's net of ride-or-die protection will be cast wider to include her. And she'll be part of the family too.

Right winger Sly Remington was high on my list of least likely ever to fall in love. The guy protects his heart the way he covers his goalie (even though Stephano Mizzoni is more than ready to defend his own honor if it comes to it.)

But I'll be honest . . .

Sometimes it's the ones you least expect to fall who take the biggest hits when love comes around.

CHAPTER 1
SLY

COASTER, PUCKS - BOTH ROUND.
WHATEVER.

"Hey, hey, there. Not without a coaster, man." Stephano Mizzoni lifted my beer and slid a little round cork puck beneath it on the bar top.

"Sorry, Mom," I quipped, catching Rock Stevens's eye and sharing a laugh.

"Don't you have any doilies you could put down, Mizzoni? I think my butt's sweating onto your barstool here," Rock added.

Mizzoni didn't crack a smile. Instead, he stepped between us, looking at us with murder in his gaze. "When you are the first in your family to own more than a shoebox, you come talk to me about how you want to take care of your things," he says, his voice low and threatening.

I clapped him on the back and picked up my beer. "No big deal man, and the place is incredible. I don't blame you for wanting to keep it pristine."

He nodded, his shoulders loosening visibly.

Rock was still chuckling, but I shot him a hard look and he zipped it.

Mizzoni had just bought the place near Wilcox, and I had to admit, it was pretty insane. Two floors of glass overlooked a back-yard pool, grounds that most national parks would envy, and an outdoor kitchen and bar nicer than most people had inside their homes. The bar was wood, but it had a glossy finish that suggested it wasn't going to be marred by one cold beer can—especially since it was built to be outside here in Virginia, where the weather was far from perfect most of the time—but it was his call to keep us in line. And while every one of these guys pushed the limit now and then, it wouldn't happen at a teammate's new house.

I sauntered across the yard, enjoying the steamy heat of the early June evening and the knowledge that we had a couple months to enjoy before we retook the ice together as the Wilcox Wombats.

If you're thinking it's an unusual name for an American pro hockey team, you're not wrong. But also, shut it. The name is distinctive, and getting on the wrong side of a whole hockey team isn't advisable.

"Sly," Chris Houstein called from one of the loungers poolside. "Where's this month's flavor?" Chris was a second-string winger, and while I loved the guy like I loved all the guys I played with, he had a big mouth.

He was sitting with Deck Gillespie and Tyler "Corny" Cornwall, soaking up the last rays of the day, margaritas in hand. I took the lounger to one side of the little group and kicked back.

"Didn't think I needed the distraction tonight. Wanted to enjoy celebrating the season with you guys." Plus, they'd recently announced a stupid "rule."

"Rock didn't get the memo," Deck said, his eyes back on the bar where Rock Stevens, our center, sat on a barstool with his fiancée Drea standing between his legs. His hand was on her ass, and the way they were making out told me they were probably minutes from slipping inside. I wondered if Mizzoni had a bunch of rules about hockey players fucking on his furniture too. Probably. But it wasn't my problem.

"Remember, fiancées are different than puck bunnies," Corny

said. "Sly didn't bring anyone because he remembers that we made a rule."

"I date a specific type of woman for a specific reason," I said. I only dated puck bunnies and other women who were interested in the lifestyle, the prominence that being seen with me brought them. There was no danger of . . . well, anything, really, if the understanding between us was clear from the start. And there was usually no drama at the end.

"Right," Deck said, slurping his margarita noisily and then eyeballing it. "These are ridiculous. I don't think Mizzoni followed the recipe when he loaded that machine he bought."

We all glanced back at the bar, where Freddy Elks and Cade Simpson were pouring another bottle of tequila into the top of the machine. "He had help," I noted.

I leaned back, letting my eyes slip shut and the sound of the music and my teammates' banter float around me. This was perfect. This was everything I needed in life.

At least it was close enough. For now.

The team would hang out here all night. Half the guys would sleep where they fell, and in the morning we'd strategize when to do it again. We'd be back at practice soon enough, but for now, we got to be just friends. A family, really. And it was one of the best feelings in the world.

Which was why it kind of sucked that I couldn't stay long, but I wasn't making my exit quite yet. I needed a few hours of this before I headed back home to face the work waiting for me there.

"You guys want to go to Europe this summer?" Deck asked.

I opened my eyes and sat up a bit. "What's your plan?"

"Thinking about renting a house or something. Someplace nice."

"Italy," Freddy suggested. "Then we get to call it a villa."

Corny sighed and didn't bother opening his eyes to say, "The Amalfi coast. But it's likely to be crowded this year since the pandemic's officially over and everything. Prices will probably go back up. I can ask my dad about the boat." Corny grew up wealthy. But not just drive-a-nice-car and have someone else clean your floors rich. His family owned islands and vineyards and probably a few small countries. Most of the time you wouldn't have known it, though.

"Shit, could you see us floating around the Mediterranean?" Deck laughed.

"Definitely," I said, wondering what the Wi-Fi would be like. Could I pull that off and still keep up my course load? Could I figure out how to get a month off from school? My phone buzzed in my pocket, interrupting my thoughts. I slid it out, happy to see Beckett's name pop up. I hadn't talked to my brother in a while, and I was pretty sure he was calling to congratulate us on a good season.

"Little brother, what's good?" I asked, a crazy sense of fulfillment washing through me. Life was pretty fucking perfect.

"I've got news, Sly." Beck sounded happy, so no alarms blared within me. We were a little worried about Dad's health, and the potential for bad news was always in the back of my mind, but it didn't sound like this was that call.

"What's going on?"

"I'm engaged, man. Zara and I are getting married."

I sat up, raising my beer to my brother, though he couldn't see it. "Congratulations, man!" I pulled the phone away from my ear and shouted, "My little brother's getting married!"

The guys all cheered and lifted drinks to toast my brother. Some of them had met Beckett, most of them hadn't. It didn't matter — this was how it was. We had each other's backs in everything. Celebrated together, mourned together.

"That's awesome," I told him. "When's the wedding?"

"Soon, actually. That's why I'm calling. Beginning of August. Think you can make it?"

I didn't even have to think about it. "Of course."

"Will you be my best man?"

"Definitely. I'm honored, little bro."

"There's, uh . . . there's just one thing." Beck said.

"What's that?"

"Mom says you can't bring one of your usual dates."

I hadn't even thought about that yet, but now I felt irritated. "Why not? What if I'm in love too?"

"Are you?"

"Of course not."

"So . . . maybe just come on your own? Unless you're really dating someone." Beck sounded hesitant, unhappy to be delivering that specific message.

"Don't worry about that, bro. You just enjoy this part of your life. I'll be there, I'll bring someone appropriate—wait, what are the bridesmaids like?"

"No."

"What do you mean, 'no'?"

"Zara's friends won't meet your requirements, anyway."

"You have no idea what my requirements are," I said, working to sound indignant.

"Let's see . . . focused on your fame, usually augmented with silicone, generally challenged when it comes to procuring clothing in appropriate sizes—"

"That's enough." I growled it, not because any of it was wrong, but because I didn't need my dating habits to be examined too closely.

"I'm sending the info via email," Beck told me. "See you soon!"

"Can't wait." I hung up, but almost as soon as I ended the call, the phone was buzzing again. Mom.

I stood and walked away from the peanut gallery next to the pool. Mom didn't need to hear any of the comments my teammates made as regularly as they breathed. "Hi Mom."

"Sylvester, honey. Great season. I'm so proud of you. Your father is over the moon."

"Thanks, Mom." It still warmed my insides to hear Mom say she was proud of me.

"Did you speak with your brother?"

"He just called."

"Isn't it wonderful? I just love Zara."

"She's great. I'm really happy for them." I was. I'd always pictured my little brother with the standard two kids and a dog, and he was on his way down that path now. It was good. Mom needed some grandkids, and they sure as hell weren't coming from me.

"And he told you the other thing?"

My good mood dampened. "I'm not bringing a date, if that's what you mean. I've been advised."

"Honey," she said, giving me her 'be reasonable' tone. "It isn't that we don't like your little girlfriends—"

"I'll just come on my own, Mom." I interrupted her before she could give me another description of my recent lady friends.

"I just . . ." Mom trailed off, and I thought I heard her sniff. "I just wish you'd work a little harder on finding the right kind of woman. Someone real. Someone who you can—"

"It's fine, Mom."

"I hate you being alone."

I laughed, and the words were out before I could really think about them. "I'm rarely alone."

"Ew."

"Sorry."

"Anyway, that's why I'm calling." She hesitated. "I have someone I want you to meet."

Alarm bells rang loud and clear in my head. "No thanks. I'm good."

"We'll see."

"Mom." I made my voice stern and low. "No setups." The last thing I needed was to break the heart or hurt the feelings of a daughter of one of Mom's friends or colleagues. Better to keep my dating habits far, far away from family.

"The engagement party is next week. I'll have your room ready. Come on Thursday. Party's on Saturday night at Shepherds." Shepherds was the fancy steakhouse inside the one upscale boutique hotel in my home town of Half Full. I could have put odds on the party being there. Of course, since Zara's parents had some cash, the whole thing could've been hijacked to wherever they lived. They weren't Corny wealthy, of course, but Zara's dad was the kind of guy who wanted you to know he did just fine.

"Okay. I'll come home Thursday."

"Can't wait to see you."

"Love you." I hung up and glanced around the yard. The barbecue was fired up, my teammates were happy and relaxed. And some of my enthusiasm for hanging out had been zapped, but I also needed to get home. I didn't like to sneak out, but I knew they wouldn't let me go, so I slipped out the side gate, hopped into my car, and headed home to study.

CHAPTER 2
CLARA

DIAGRAMS ARE EDUCATIONAL

"This day has gone to shit."

"Tell me about it," my best friend Andie laughed on the other end of the phone.

"No. Seriously. I'm covered in bear shit."

"You are the only person who can say that, you know. I mean, the only person who can say it and actually mean that you are literally covered in shit."

"Well, that's something, I guess. I do mean it somewhat figuratively too." I was almost back to my truck, which was the only reason I had any service at all. It had been a brutally long day in the field, and I was hot, and sticky. And covered in . . . well, you got it.

"Hey, what are you up to tonight?" Andie had this way of asking about my plans with a lilt in her voice that made it sound like she had something absolutely incredible up her sleeve, like if I only said yes, my whole life would change.

"Showering. Picking up Katie. Probably not in that order, though."

"What if . . ." she drew this out, and I knew she thought she was going to have to convince me about whatever it was. I unlocked the truck and slid in behind the wheel, starting it up and doing my best to sync Andie's pause with the natural pause caused by the phone switching to the car speaker. "What do you think?"

"Sorry. Missed that." As I pulled the truck out onto the highway, my exhaustion sank in. We'd been tracking a couple momma bears for a few days, and had finally gotten one of them collared late this afternoon. The rest of the crew had been just steps ahead of me pulling out and heading home. I needed some sleep.

"I said, what do you think about hitting the new club downtown? I got us on the VIP list."

Oh god. That sounded legitimately awful. The groan I let out must've given away my complete lack of desire to shove myself into tight pants and then suffer through inappropriate come-on lines all night while doing my best to drink enough to handle the overwhelming insanity of a club while not drinking so much that I'd collapse from sheer exhaustion. Plus, there was Katie.

"Andie, I can't tonight. I'm like the walking dead. I need sleep."

I could practically hear the pout on the other end of the phone. "But you're my wingwoman and I need to get laid."

"Don't we all?" I laughed. Andie and I had been best friends since high school, and we'd both followed the detour into the land of totally ill-advised marriages and having babies before we could gracefully handle a shot of tequila. The only difference now? She was really good at tequila.

"So, here's our chance!"

"Honestly," I told her as I navigated the highway offramp and headed toward home, "if the opportunity arose tonight, I'd probably sleep through it. Besides, I'm kind of tired of random hookups. There are no decent guys around Half Full. We've met them all."

"That's why a new club might mean fresh meat!"

"Hon . . ."

"I know. I can hear in your voice how tired you are. Maybe tomorrow?"

I thought about it. "I don't think I can ask Mrs. Remington for another night. Plus, the whole strategy behind raising reasonable humans is actually spending some time with them, I think. Katie already throws a fit every time I take her next door."

"Yeah," Andie said, finally giving in. "Katie deserves some mom time."

"You could come hang out with us soon?"

"Definitely! Pizza and Auntie Andie night? Stella too?"

"Of course! Let me know when you can. I understand if you'd rather get laid though, I know you've got those handy parents to babysit."

She sighed. "Nah, we'd always rather hang out with you guys. You're more fun."

"If we're more fun than getting laid, there's a chance you're doing it wrong. I'll draw you a picture next time I see you."

"Funny."

I pulled into my driveway, ignoring the slightly stagnant feeling that always came over me as I did, like a form of deja vu that didn't get realized. I'd lived in this house my entire life, with the exception of the four years I was away for school, the two years my rapidly fizzling marriage had lasted, and a few years while I tried to raise Katie on my own and help my failing parents. But my parents were gone, so now the house was mine.

"Night, friend," I told Andie, idling in the driveway, switching off the light.

"Night. Love you."

"Same."

I switched off the truck, ending the call, and then did a quick sniff check. Pretty bad, but Mrs. Remington had definitely seen me at my worst, considering she'd lived next door my whole life. She'd witnessed my serious acne phase, the poorly planned perm phase, and also that phase we do not discuss. The one where I was in love with her son and made a complete fool of myself on the daily through two full years of high school.

But those days were over. We'd all moved on, and now she

was the cheapest and most capable babysitter I had. And I needed to thank her, get Katie, and get us both to bed.

I locked the truck and headed to the doorstep next door, stamping my feet on the lawn as I went, in hopes of getting most of the forest debris and muck off before I tracked it up her steps.

"There you are," Mrs. Remington cried, pulling the door open before I could knock.

"I'm so sorry to be late. Again."

"Oh, honey, you know I don't mind at all. You and Katie just make my days! Heaven knows Sam isn't much fun these days."

I could hear the television blaring from the front room where Mr. Remington liked to watch whatever sports were on, with little regard for team loyalty or preference. Unless it was hockey, of course. Then he only rooted for the Wombats. For good reason.

"Well, I sure appreciate your help. I wish there was some way I could repay you. I honestly don't know what I'd do without you." It was the same conversation we had almost every time I picked Katie up. Only tonight, Mrs. Remington had a strange look on her face, a kind of half smile twinned with a little upturn of her rosy lips on one side. She looked uncertain, and devious.

"Actually, Clara . . . there is a little something I was hoping you'd be willing to do."

I was exhausted, but I owed this woman. So. Much. "Sure," I said, coaxing some energy into my voice. "What is it?"

"Just a little favor of your time is all."

"I'm happy to help," I told her.

She clapped her hands just as Katie appeared next to her, poking her blond head out to the side of Mrs. Remington's legs. "Hi Mommy."

"Hey Katie-bear. How was your night?"

"Good," Katie smiled. "We made krispy treats."

"Fun," I said, reaching for the little girl who made the sun and moon rise and fall in my world. She moved into my arms and I hoisted her onto my hip.

"You smell poopy."

I buried my nose in her hair for a few breaths and let out a laugh that was more of a sigh. "I know. Sorry, baby."

"No, it's okay. You smell like you."

And there it was. I was the mommy who usually smelled like bear shit. This was my life.

"We should get going to bed. And to shower," I told Mrs. Remington.

"So we'll see you Thursday night?"

"Thursday? Sorry?"

"You said you wanted to repay me."

"Oh, right." I was happy to help her out with whatever. She probably needed some help moving the boxes she'd been mentioning in the attic over the garage. "Happy to help. What time?"

"Six o'clock should be good." She smiled, and I caught another glimpse of that look, but was too tired to consider it. "Dress up a little. We'll have dinner."

Oh. Dinner. Maybe she was just lonely, seeing as how Sam rarely moved out of his chair by the TV since having a heart attack a few months back. "Um, sure. See you then," I told her, turning with my arms full of little girl.

I could feel her watching us head to our house as she stood on the doorstep until we were safely inside. That was the kind of people the Remingtons were. The kind that cared enough to see you safely inside your house. Most of them were like that, at least.

CHAPTER 3

SLY

FACE OFF WITH A SPIDER MONKEY

By the time Thursday rolled around, I was in a good place. I'd managed to turn in an essay and had just wrapped a group project that was due Friday. I had a lecture tonight that I was going to miss, but there was little chance it was going to be important, since we'd just turned in a project. I didn't blow off school often, but I felt pretty confident that missing this one lecture wouldn't be a big deal.

So I headed home for the weekend with a clear schedule and only twelve months to go before I could throw some fancy initials after my name. And those letters? They were my insurance plan. The team owner, Steve Rhinolakis—who we obviously called "Rhino"—had confided he was on the hunt for a business manager slash head of finance, and that he hoped maybe one day he could step away. I'd mentioned to him once that I was looking for something as a next step, and he convinced me that I'd be a contender, though heaven only knew why. The MBA was his only reservation, so I'd promised to make it happen. I didn't know if I wanted to actually own the Wombats eventually, but I did know that hockey was my past, present, and future. And if I couldn't play, I could at least find a way to stay close.

But right now I needed to head home. Alone.

As if I would have taken a date to Mom and Dad's house to stay. First of all, that would have broken one of my rules for dating, which was that you never got into a situation where you couldn't easily say goodbye if things took a turn. And sharing my childhood bedroom out of town? That would just be complicated. And possibly awkward.

Besides, my family had been pretty clear.

I thought about their request as I drove, feeling slightly more irritated about it with each passing mile.

But I suspected the annoyance I was feeling came more from knowing they were right than from being told not to bring anyone. I dated people I knew would never turn into anything serious. Things were easier that way, and I liked keeping the lines clear. Plus, I had no illusions about the things women liked about me. The athletic skill, the status, the money, the muscles. Maybe not in that order.

It was a gorgeous blue-sky day as I pulled into the driveway at Mom and Dad's house. The green lawns of the neighborhood lined up like squares on a Monopoly board, each one exactly like the others. The driveways formed a series of parallel lines, the uniformity of the scene challenged only by the enormous trees that grew near the curb, arching out to drape the street in shade.

This neighborhood was old and quaint, and the second I drove into it, a deep sense of nostalgia filled my gut. This was home. This was childhood and high school. I couldn't stop myself from imagining Mom's SUV, stuffed to the gills with hockey gear, parked in the driveway.

Of course she didn't drive that car anymore. Ten years of carting me and Beckett and all our sports gear around had left the thing with a permanent funk, and as soon as I'd gone pro, I bought her the Tesla she'd had her eye on.

Lots of things had changed, but some hadn't. As I guided my car past Mom's prized hydrangeas, my eyes wandered to the little blue house next door and I did my best not to dwell on thoughts of Clara Connor.

I hadn't seen her in years. Beckett said she got married and moved away, but it was hard not to picture her sitting on the front steps with her friend—what was that girl's name? Andrea? Amy?—and laughing as they watched the neighborhood go by. Sometimes, when I was feeling particularly alone, I could almost conjure the sound. It was full and light, like sunshine and bubbles and something so, so sexy all wrapped together.

Mom told me recently that Clara's folks had died a year ago, but last I heard the house was empty. I imagined Clara was living a happy life somewhere else, with her husband and family. Man, she was hot. An old crush simmered inside me as I considered the brainy girl next door.

I parked, pulling the keys from the ignition, and stepped out of the car to inhale the familiar scents of the neighborhood in summer. Some kind of flowery musk hung in the air, and I didn't know what it was, but it made me think of swimming pools and long summer days. I grabbed my backpack and my duffel, and headed to the front door.

"There he is!" Mom threw the door open as I raised my hand to try the knob, and a second later, she was wrapping her arms around my middle, hugging me for all she was worth.

"Hey Mom," I chuckled, doing my best to hug her back without dropping all my stuff.

"It's so good to have you home." She stepped back, looking up at me with shining eyes.

"You know I live less than two hours away. You guys can come visit any time."

"I know." She swatted me. "Come inside, come on. Your brother and Zara are in the living room with Dad."

I could hear a baseball game blaring from the living room, and I dropped my bags by the door and followed Mom inside. Dad was in his recliner, and Beckett and Zara were on the couch, sharing some intimate whispered conversation, which Mom interrupted by shouting, "Look who's here!"

Dad pointed the remote at the TV, quieting the noise, and Beck and Zara rose to their feet.

Beckett had done well for himself where his fiancée was concerned. Zara was smart and funny, and gorgeous on top of that. I was happy for him. My little brother deserved the best.

"Hey guys," I kissed Zara on the cheek as I gave her a gentle squeeze, and then I hugged Beck, making sure to pick him up and shake him a little bit when I did it.

"Hey!" he protested as I squeezed him a bit harder than I needed to, and as soon as his feet hit the ground, he did a quick swipe of my wrist, stepped sideways and pulled me into a choke-hold. Fucking Aikido.

"Oh no you don't!" I locked my arms around his waist as soon as he let go, and we danced around like that for at least a minute, both of us shouting profanities as we put Mom's living room trinkets in mortal danger.

"Twatwaffle!" Beckett yelled as I stomped on his bare foot.

"Turkey dick!" I responded when he tried to lift a knee into my family jewels.

"Knock it off, you assholes!" Dad was on his feet, and Beck and I immediately dropped our arms and stepped apart. It took a lot to get Dad out of the recliner, and we'd been well trained.

"Sorry, sir," Beckett muttered, narrowing his eyes at me.

"Hey Dad. Sorry." I stepped closer to Dad, and his hand shot out to shake mine.

"I was going to tell you how proud I was of you. Before you and your brother reverted back to elementary school."

"Sorry," I said again. "We can't help it."

"Try," Dad said sternly, glaring between us. Then his shoulders relaxed slightly and he grinned. "Great season, Sylvester."

My parents were the only people who didn't call me Sly. Them, and Beck when he was trying to piss me off.

"Thanks, Dad. Next year we'll get the cup." We'd gotten close, but the damn Roosters had beat us in the playoffs. Still made me grumpy to think about.

"Come into the kitchen for a drink," Mom suggested, and when Dad moved back toward his chair, she gave him her angry-Mom voice. "You too, Sam."

Dad shrugged, and we all headed to the kitchen, where Mom announced the cocktail of the evening. Ever since I was a kid, Mom had been trying out new cocktail recipes and subjecting us to them. I really would have preferred a beer, but tonight I was presented with something blue in a martini glass instead.

"We have to drink them in here or take them outside. These will stain the carpet," Mom said when each of us stood in the kitchen awkwardly holding a glass of blue liquid.

"Let's go outside then, so we can at least sit down, Violet." Dad was frowning, but his voice held that same hint of amusement it always did when he was talking to Mom. Or about her. She was quirky, and she kept him from becoming the grumpy and impossible man he was evidently bred to be. It had always been this way, and seeing them together, seeing that nothing had changed, made me feel that same sense of nostalgia I'd gotten driving back into the neighborhood.

We headed out, and Mom pulled the screen on the back door.

"You're gonna let the AC out, Violet."

"I want to be able to hear the doorbell is all." Mom smiled, but didn't say anything else as the scent of some devious plan wafted by on the breeze. I sipped my drink, realizing that it was most likely related to Beck and Zara, or possibly, to me. Nothing for it. Mom was Mom.

We arranged ourselves on the patio, and held our glasses aloft, toasting my brother and Zara.

"I'm really happy for you guys," I told them. "Congratulations."

The way Zara smiled at my brother before we each sipped the blue atrocities Mom had made caused a little surge of something to poke me in the gut, but I did my best to drown whatever it was with blue stuff.

"What is this?" I asked, halfway through what tasted like a melted Slurpee with a kick.

"It's a Blue Hawaiian. Good, isn't it?" Mom looked so pleased with herself, I had to agree.

"These are really yummy, Mrs. Remington," Zara said, sipping hers delicately. "Thank you so much for going to all the trouble."

"No trouble at all," Mom beamed, and then she added. "Darling, will you please call me Violet? Mrs. Remington makes me feel so old."

Zara was about to answer when an unholy screech rent the air around us.

"What the hell?" I asked, rising and looking around.

The sound came again, drifting from the front of the house, and this time it formed actual words, "no no no NOOOO."

I headed inside, depositing my glass on the counter as I moved toward the front door to investigate. Whatever it was sounded like it was on our doorstep.

I pulled open the front door just as the sound came again, and I immediately identified the source. The most adorable little girl—all pink dress and perky blond ponytails—stood on the front step, and the ungodly sound was coming from her mouth.

I took a step back from the noise as I looked up at the face of the person whose leg she was currently wrapped around, and my heart did some kind of irritating double beat thing.

Clara Connor.

"Hi," she said, her husky voice sounding exactly like it did in my memory. Or what I could hear of it over the screaming, at least.

Mom had joined me at the door by then, and she was grinning from ear to ear.

"Clara, I'm so glad you could come."

The adorable hellion at her feet screamed louder when she spotted Mom.

"I don't want you to goooooooo!" The tiny person wrapped herself tighter around Clara's leg, which was draped in a floral skirt, connected to a sundress that was currently being tugged very low in the front and forcing me to struggle to avert my gaze. Clara gave Mom a smile and then reached down for the person attached to her and pried the little girl off from her leg, squatting and holding her at arm's distance.

"I told you, I'm not going anywhere. We're both staying for dinner."

"Hello there, Katie," Mom cooed. "I have purple Play-doh and I made you a very special grown-up drink just like the one I have for your mommy." Mom did not look the least bit ruffled by the little girl's bright red face or clear disdain at being brought to her house for the evening.

As Mom spoke to Katie, my eyes found Clara's face.

She looked good. Her blond hair fell in waves around her face, and her skin was tanned and glowing. The sharp blue eyes I remembered snagged on my own, and a jolt of attraction hit me hard.

"Hey Sly," she said, and I thought I saw a faint blush crawl up her cheeks under the tan.

"Clara. Long time no see." Idiot. Who said that?

She smiled, but the expression dropped almost immediately. "Yeah, um, Violet, I don't know if we can stay."

"We can't stay!" the little girl—Katie, I guessed—shrieked at us.

"Oh, don't be silly. Katie and I are friends," Mom said, moving aside and waving Clara and Katie in.

The little girl was now clamped around Clara's neck and shoulders, and her eyes found my face as Clara moved inside, carrying her. They went wide as we made eye contact, and then narrowed, and I could see the next scream before it emerged from her tiny body.

"Nooooo!" That one felt personal, because it was delivered almost directly at me.

"I'm so sorry," Clara was saying to Mom as the tiny person eyeballed me like we were about to face off over a puck. "I think

I've just been working a lot and whenever we come this way she thinks I'm leaving her."

"Then this will be good for both of you," Mom said as we moved into the kitchen. Mom seemed weirdly unperturbed, and I wondered if we wouldn't be better off just to let them go home.

"I just don't know if she's going to be reasonable," Clara said, sounding exhausted. "This phase has been . . . tough. Moving again, and my parents . . ."

"Oh, honey. I know." Mom gave Clara's arm a little pat and then turned back to the counter, where she was fixing Clara a drink.

The little girl was clutched onto Clara like a spider monkey, her little hands leaving red marks on Clara's skin that had my mind going to places it definitely shouldn't venture, and for a second the girl's accusing gaze made me feel like she knew exactly what I was thinking.

That Clara Connor was still the hottest thing I'd ever seen. That I'd like to mark up her skin, and then kiss away the marks. Maybe lick them . . .

Man, the woman did it for me. She always had . . .

"Hi," I said to the irate being in Clara's arms.

The little face shifted slightly, an eyebrow raising as she regarded me while her mother and mine discussed the blue drinks Mom was pouring.

I raised a hand and gave her a little wave.

She continued eyeballing me suspiciously, but lifted her chin from Clara's shoulder.

I made a face, crossing my eyes and wrinkling my nose, and then stopped, gauging her reaction.

She looked confused.

I would be too, if a grown man started making weird faces at me. But here we were.

Now I did a little dance, shimmying back and forth and giving her another face.

That made her smile, and I felt like I'd scored, glee washing through me.

It was time to go full throttle, I decided as Mom explained to Clara how long she'd been working on this cocktail recipe to get it just right. I broke into a full boogie, rolling my hands in front of me and shaking my hips, my shoulders going in time. It was a dance I wouldn't be caught dead doing in a club, or really, anywhere. But it made this tiny person laugh, and suddenly I felt like a hero, like I could do just about anything.

Until Clara spun around and caught me.

I stopped immediately and cleared my throat, but a tiny smile lifted the side of her mouth too, and the victory I'd secured with her daughter escalated in my chest. It felt good to make her smile.

"Sylvester," my mother said, oblivious to the scene going on a moment before. "You remember Clara Connor from next door."

"Yeah, of course," I managed, greeting her a second time for Mom's benefit.

"And this is Beckett's older brother," Mom told Clara as if she'd have no idea who I was.

"I remember," she said, that honey sandpaper voice doing something to my gut again. "How are you doing, Sylvester?"

"Good, yeah. Call me Sly, okay?"

She blushed again and I wanted to toss her over my shoulder and carry her into my bedroom. I stuffed my hands in my pockets instead.

"Your name is Siiiilllll-veeeessssst-errrr?" the little girl had swung around to keep her eyes on me, and my name seemed to amuse her greatly.

It kind of pissed me off.

"People call me Sly," I told her, more defensive than I should have been, given her size and age.

"That's weird."

"Katie, that's not nice," Clara said.

"Your name is Kaaaaaattiiiiiieeeee?" I asked her, and Mom

tsked next to me as my maturity level dropped to match my current opponent.

"It's Katherine," she sniffed, lifting her little chin as her mother put her feet on the floor.

"Fancy," I noted.

She frowned at me. "Do you live here? I've never seen you here."

"You here a lot?" I shot back.

Mom stepped between us, clearly feeling like this little showdown needed to come to an end. "I babysit for Katie while Clara works late sometimes," she said, forcing a blue drink into Clara's hand. "We're all out on the patio, dear." Then she bent over, looking Katie in the eye. "Do you want a blue drink too?"

"Okay," Katie said eagerly, suddenly dropping the indignant act and following Mom to the counter.

"The kid probably doesn't need a Blue Hawaiian, Mom," I said, grabbing a beer from the refrigerator.

"It's Blue Hawaiian punch," Mom said, handing a plastic martini glass to Katie, who smirked at me as she followed Mom back outside.

I opened the beer in the now-quiet kitchen and took a long swig, trying to build my defenses back up after the double assault of seeing Clara again and being called to the mat by her daughter.

It was going to be a long night.

CHAPTER 4

CLARA

DIRTY CANDY

I left the kitchen with Violet and Katie, heading for the small group gathered on the patio.

"Clara!" Beckett greeted me, friendly and cheerful as ever.

"Hey Beckett." I returned the warm smile he offered as Violet waved me toward a padded rattan chair facing a low coffee table where the others sat.

"So great to see you, and Katie. Hello," he said, softer now, looking at my daughter who was pretending to be shy, ducking behind Violet as they joined the group.

"Katie, you know Beckett. You can say hello." I met her eyes and gave her a meaningful look.

"Hi," she whispered.

"And I'd like to introduce you both to Zara," Beck said, his hand reaching to that of the beautiful dark-haired woman in the chair next to him. "My fiancée."

"Oh my gosh, congratulations," I said, gushing a little bit because I really did just love love. And they looked so happy, sitting there, beaming at one another. "That's wonderful."

"Good to see you again, Clara," Sam said, more personable now that he was detached from his recliner and the television.

"You too, Sir. Thanks for inviting me over."

Katie had managed to gain a bright blue mustache in the few minutes since we'd left the kitchen, and now she abandoned her blue punch to hover behind my chair. I could feel, more than see, that she was taken with Zara beside me. It was hard not to be. There was something magnetic about the small woman with the dark eyes.

"Are you tired of telling the 'how we met' story?" I asked her and Beck.

She laughed, "Not at all."

"I haven't heard it either." Sly's deep voice rumbled from somewhere behind me, and I did my best not to react, but my body had a will of its own where he was concerned. I wished it wasn't true. It would have made life so much easier in high school, but I didn't seem to be able to help that I was ridiculously attracted to the man. He was only the first in a string of ill-suited men that my libido seemed to fixate on.

I was older now, though. More mature, certainly. I could hold my own here. I steeled myself.

And then he took the chair on my other side, and the subtle scent of something smoky and soft hit me, teasing my senses. He smelled like caramel and leather—and the combination twisted up my insides and muddled my brain.

Damn Sylvester Remington. Why couldn't I ignore this man?

"You smell like dirty candy," Katie told him, clearly having overcome any uncertainty where he was concerned.

Beckett burst into laughter, and I took Katie's hand, pulling her to sit on my lap. "We don't comment on how people smell," I whispered.

I glanced at Sly, who looked amused by her pronouncement as he took a swig of his beer.

"Why don't you tell us all the story, dear?" Violet suggested to Beckett.

"Sure," he said, draping an arm over Zara's shoulders.

He told the story about how they'd met at work where Zara

had actually started out as Beck's boss, eventually moving to another department when it became clear they wanted to be together. As the story unfolded, I became increasingly aware of something going on between my daughter and the hulking being on my other side.

Katie was alternately stiffening and then relaxing into a pile of little-girl giggles, and without even looking, I could tell that Sly was entertaining her somehow.

I glanced over at him, preparing myself to catch whatever was going on between them, but he gave me a wide-eyed innocent look and mouthed, "What?"

Turning my attention back to Zara and Beck, I tried not to focus on Sylvester Remington, but it was impossible.

Sly had always done things to me that I couldn't explain, stirred parts of me that no one else seemed able to touch. The fact that I'd had an out-of-control crush on him in high school hadn't mattered to him in the least, however. He was too busy being a hockey god and getting any girl he wanted with a simple lift of his perfect clefted chin.

And the girls he wanted were nothing like me.

Honestly, my fixation on Sly had been exhausting. And demoralizing. And there was no way in hell I was ever going there again. But since my body seemed completely oblivious to the danger, I knew I'd have to take some kind of action to protect myself. And my daughter, who clearly had the same Sly Remington gene that I did, based on the way she was melting at whatever it was he was doing.

I turned to him again, and made my face stern. "I don't know what you're doing, but stop it," I said.

Sly raised his hands again, playing innocent. "She started it."

"Well, you're being rude, which is totally up to you, but Katie is just learning her manners, and you're setting a poor example." I leaned into my daughter's ear, wrenching my eyes from the handsome face. "When someone is talking, you should be giving them your attention." I turned my body and hers to face Zara, who was finishing up the story of how she and the younger Remington brother had become engaged.

"And that was how it began," she said, her smile lighting her dark eyes in a way that spoke of sheer contentment.

I'd felt that way once. Or I thought I had. But I doubted I'd ever looked quite as certain as Zara and Beck did. Katie's dad had never inspired certainty. His entire purpose seemed to be to keep me from getting too comfortable. I'd spent three years letting him tell me who to be and how to be before it had finally become clear to both of us that I would never be what he wanted. And he didn't want Katie either, as it turned out. The idea of a wife and daughter had been all Zach wanted. Faced with the realities of conflict and diapers, he'd bailed. My stomach rolled at the memory of living in that situation.

"The engagement dinner is Saturday," Beckett told me. "We'd love it if you'd come. Both of you."

"Is it dress up?" Katie asked, her little voice full of excitement.

"It is," Zara confirmed. Then she looked up at me. "Nothing too fancy. We're just having dinner over at Shepherds."

"It's so nice of you to invite us," I said, my mind working to find a polite way to say no thank you. One night of trying to ignore Sly was going to be enough, certainly.

"Wonderful," Violet clapped her hands as if it had been decided, and then rose. "Sam, could you join me in the kitchen please? Dinner will just be a minute," she told the rest of us.

They went back inside, and I took a too-big sip of my blue drink, looking for a way to defuse the discomfort I felt sitting so close to Sly. It was like there was some kind of radiation coming out of the man next to me, and even as I tried to ignore him, it was pinging off my skin, affecting me whether I wanted it to or not.

"Beck says you're a biologist?" Zara said, her wide smile aimed at me.

"Mommy is a wildlife boologist," Katie told her.

"BI-ologist," I corrected automatically, then I laughed, meeting Zara's eyes. "Yeah, I am."

"That must be so interesting," she said.

"What does that mean, exactly?" The deep voice came from behind me. I'd turned to face Zara, scooting to the edge of my chair, basically turning my back on Sly.

"Um, it . . ." I swiveled back, and finally half stood with Katie still on my lap, pushing the chair back so I could see everyone at once. I also put a little more distance between myself and him. It was almost like our chairs had been arranged close together on purpose. "I work for the state," I told them. "And the program I'm most involved with focuses on the black bear population in the Piedmont region."

"What do you mean?" Beckett asked, his face full of interest.

I knew that if I got going, I'd be talking long after anyone cared. My work was my passion, but it wasn't everyone's, I knew it definitely hadn't been Zach's, so I tried to be succinct. "Well, there are a few areas of focus. First, we try to keep tabs on the population, to understand the resources they're using and track their migration pattern. Bears have descended from the Western mountains and now range through most of the state. That's happened over the last twenty years or so," I told them. "But the main focus of my work is tracking breeding females and cubs."

"Mommy finds homes for orphans," Katie declared, and then appeared to have had enough of my job. She bolted from my lap and darted out into the wide grassy expanse of the back yard to spin in circles under the evening sky.

"Orphans," Sly repeated. "Bear orphans?"

"Right." My voice faltered when I met his interested eyes, and I quickly shifted my attention back to his brother. Safer territory. "Each season, we take in orphaned cubs, and part of my work involves rehoming them with mothers already raising babies."

"Oh my gosh," Zara breathed. "That's so interesting. So you just, like, drop the babies off and the mom accepts them?"

"Kind of," I said, nodding. "We have a pretty good idea which females are likely to adopt, and those are the ones we'll try. And yeah, we just kind of sneak the baby in with the other cubs."

"Isn't that dangerous?" Sly asked, sounding kind of pissed off.

I glanced at him, confirming that he looked mad too. I had a chilling memory of a similar discussion with Zach. "Um. Yeah, it can be. We're pretty careful."

"You have a kid."

My eyes touched Katie, assuring that she was okay, and then found his face again. He was frowning, but there was something in his disapproval I'd never felt with Zach. Like Sly was being protective. I sensed his point, but also didn't need my high school crush weighing in on the appropriateness of my career choice. "I see your observation skills have improved since we were in high school."

He frowned. "What's that mean?"

"Maybe not your intelligence, though." I rose, wishing I hadn't said the words out loud as Beckett burst into laughter. I headed out to the lawn to join Katie, though she clearly didn't need me. Mostly, I needed to get away from Sly. Without consulting me, my brain had obviously decided that the best defense would be a good offense, and now I'd been rude to my host's son.

"Dinner is ready!" Violet called out the back door.

I busied myself helping Katie get her hands washed and get to the table in the dining room where Violet showed us our places, studiously avoiding eye contact with Sly, who I could feel watching me as we entered the dining room.

"Here you go," Violet said, waving me into a chair at his side.

"Oh, um . . ." I couldn't exactly demand to sit somewhere else.

"Have a seat," he growled. "I'll try not to let my lack of intellect ruin your meal."

Shit. I turned to him. "Sorry about that," I said.

He lifted a shoulder, his face revealing nothing. I doubted it was possible to hurt the feelings of a guy like him. He'd been named sexiest man on the ice by some regional magazine, after all, and I'd seen a profile on national television about him. The opinion of some girl from his small-town past surely didn't bother him. And it wasn't like I actually meant it, anyway. I'd tutored him in math for a little while one year, and he was every bit as intelligent as anyone else.

The rest of the meal was tense. Sam hardly spoke, and Beckett and Zara seemed to be always in secret communication between the two of them, sharing some love language no one else was in on. Katie was busy slurping spaghetti noodles one by one. No matter what I did, she insisted on eating noodles this way. Sly held himself stiffly at my side, and every time I glanced at him, his face was stony and hard.

"I think it's going to be just beautiful," Violet was saying. She'd been describing the venue for the wedding through most of the meal, not seeming bothered that her table mates were all preoccupied with other things. "There are tiny cabins, all situated around the lake, and the main lodge is just gorgeous. Very chic, really, for a rustic resort."

"That'll be so nice," I said.

Violet beamed at me.

"So Katie lives with her dad while you go out hunting bears?" The question came from Sly in a voice so low it was practically a vibration between us.

I frowned at him. "No. Katie really doesn't see her dad."

"Why not?"

This guy really had no boundaries. "That's not your business."

He met my eyes then, narrowing his gaze as if he'd be able to see the answer if he just focused hard enough. "Hmmm."

I put down the piece of garlic bread I'd been holding. "Hmmm? What? You want to pass another judgment on a life you know nothing about?" I whispered this, not wanting to involve the entire table in whatever was happening between me and Sly Remington.

"Sorry, do you have a monopoly on that?"

I shook my head, holding his dark-eyed gaze. "What?"

His eyes stayed locked on mine, and the rest of the room faded away as our focus melded together. I wouldn't have been surprised to find smoke rising from between us, since the intensity of the look was turning my insides to some kind of unrecognizable mush, and my brain was stuttering in my head. And then, with what felt like effort, he pulled his attention away and stuffed a huge bite of pasta into his mouth, leaving me to practically collapse against the back of my chair.

Crap. Whatever fascination I'd held for this guy was clearly still there. Only now, he seemed intent on playing with me. Or pissing me off. I couldn't tell what his motivation was, I just knew I needed to stay away from him.

Sly Remington was bad news, and I didn't have time for it.

CHAPTER 5
SLY

IT'S NEVER OKAY TO BE A DICK

I did my best to stay quiet the rest of the meal because every time I opened my mouth, horrendous surprises issued forth like demon spawn. Still, Clara continued to ignore me right up through Mom's dessert, through coffee, and even as she and Katie thanked everyone and headed for the front door.

I'd almost made it to the end of the evening when Mom said, "So we'll see you on Saturday for the party. Sly will pick you both up."

"What?" I thought I'd whispered, but it might have come out as something more like a growl.

"No, that's—" Clara began to protest and I was equal parts relieved and disappointed. I didn't want to see her again. And I wanted to see her again so badly I thought it was possible my life would never be quite the same again if I didn't.

"We insist," Mom told her. And when Mom insisted, that was pretty much it, unless you wanted to be cleaning toilets for the next two months or performing some other menial chore as punishment. Clara didn't know that, though.

"I'll definitely look at my calendar," she was saying. "I'm just not sure if—"

"Mooommmmmyyyyy." I couldn't suppress the smile that

Katie's pleading voice inspired. That kid. Something about her, man.

"Okay, well, I'll let you know," Clara said, though I couldn't see her from where I was basically hiding in the dining room around the corner from the front door.

"Sly will be by at five-thirty Saturday," Mom told her as if Clara had said none of the things she'd just said.

"See you then!" Katie cried loudly. "Thank you for dinner!" Her volume was cranked to eleven. She'd be great at a hockey game.

As the front door shut, I lifted my eyes from the floorboards in front of me to find Beck still sitting at the table in the next room, watching me with an exceedingly irritating expression on his face.

"Shut it," I said, hoping to preempt any dumbfuckery about to come from that direction.

"Seriously, man. What was all that?" Beck shook his head slowly back and forth, a smile spreading across his face.

I sniffed. "Fuck off."

He laughed.

I really wanted to punch him. The whole night had gotten under my skin somehow. Between Katie being both ridiculously cute and highly obnoxious all in one teeny tiny little blonde package and Clara appearing like my high school wet dream all grown up and even sexier . . . I was not quite myself. I needed time to recombobulate.

"I'm working this one out," Beck said, leaning back in his chair and picking up his coffee cup. "And I think I'm close. Either you have a serious hard-on for our next-door neighbor, or you've taken more hits to the head than I realized this season. Or you're just a total dick."

"Let's go with the last one, asshole." I stood, pushing my chair back and hoping to just slip away, back to the bedroom I'd occupied until college, where I could finally put enough distance between me and the house next door to think straight.

"Sly, have you ever heard the expression 'you catch more flies with honey than with vinegar?'" Beck asked, following me.

I turned around and glared down at him. "Have you ever heard the expression 'mind your own business or I'll pound you into the ground?'"

"No," he said. "You sure you're getting it right? Not familiar."

I was twenty kinds of annoyed and angry and I didn't even know what else. Of course I'd thought about the house next door every time I'd been home over the years . . . But she had never been there. She wasn't supposed to be there. "I'm going to bed," I told my brother. "I'll see you in the morning."

"Okay, Romeo," he said, turning away with a smug smile and heading back toward the family room where Dad had baseball blaring once again.

Back in my own room, I dropped to the bed, stretching out to stare at the familiar crack in the ceiling as I pieced through whatever the fuck had happened out there.

I'd been fine. My usual charming self.

And then the little blond imp had challenged me the second she'd walked through the door, at a moment when I was not quite balanced, thanks to the sudden appearance of Clara Connor.

I'd tried to wrap my head around this grown-up version of Clara while Katie had continued trying to get my goat. Which she totally did, by the way. Hell, she got the entire herd.

Crap, now I was thinking in farmyard analogies. I was fucked.

I needed to get back to Wilcox quick, fast, and in a hurry, and ground myself in what I was good at. Hockey. Maybe the only thing I was good at.

But I wondered if even two hours of winding highway was enough to erase from my brain the knowledge that Clara Connor was single again. And so fucking pretty and smart that sitting next to her made me feel completely inadequate in the most horribly familiar way.

I blew out a slow breath, doing my best to get a grip on the raging emotions engaged in a cage fight inside my chest. What the hell was wrong with me?

I picked up my phone and dialed, relieved when the call was answered on the first ring.

"Sly."

"Rock."

"It's fairly late."

"But you answered the phone."

"Sly, this is why we have a team shrink. Or psychologist, or whatever."

"Don't need her. Just a new point of view. From a friend." Rock and I had been friends for years, though since he'd hooked up with Drea, our friendship had felt a bit more like me calling him and him sometimes answering.

"What's up, man?" he sighed, and I thought I heard him sit down to listen.

I called Rock when I had decisions to make, or when there were things going on inside me that I couldn't piece through. Like now. Rock wasn't as good as the team psych, but he also didn't make me feel like an idiot.

I explained everything that had happened from the moment I'd walked through the front door this afternoon.

"Let me see," Rock said, his carrying a hint of amusement that made me wonder the wisdom of calling him. "You're back in your childhood home. And you ran into and then had dinner at your mom's with the chick who broke your heart in high school."

"I mean, that's a bit of a stretch, the heart-breaking part."

"Is it?"

I frowned, but Rock couldn't see me. Not that my mad face would intimidate him in the least. "Maybe not."

"Put it in context, though. We all remember the girl we had it bad for in high school. I think it's some hormonal shit you don't get over."

"And what do I do?"

"Going home has got to bring back some other kinds of

nostalgia too, right? Maybe you're just kind of wrapped up in all of that."

That made sense. "Okay." Maybe she didn't affect me that much. Maybe it was just being home and stuff.

"So you were already off balance. And then you saw her, and it was like total deja vu."

"Yes. That sounds right. So why was I such a dick?"

"You reverted. Makes sense."

"It does? So it's okay that I was a dick?"

"It's never okay to be a dick." Shit. He was right.

"So what do I do now?"

"You seeing her again?" Rock asked.

"Mom told her I'd pick her up and take her to my brother's engagement party on Saturday." The very thought of it made my insides flip around like a half-dead trout.

"Then you'll have a do-over. That's good. Just apologize."

I didn't like the sound of that. I did not like to apologize. Especially when I wasn't sure I'd done anything really wrong. She'd been kind of rude too, after all. "Do you think she's going to apologize, though?"

"For what?"

"For . . . I thought back over the course of the evening. "She called me unobservant and unintelligent."

"Well, she might, I guess. Doesn't matter though. You can only control yourself and the way you react to shit. That's what our work together is all about."

"Right." I did not want to apologize. But I would.

Because I was a grown-ass man who was in control of the way he reacted to things. Things like crazy-hot women who wrestled bears for work and produced tiny blond people with smart mouths and twinkling little eyes and the best laughs I'd ever heard. And Clara Connor couldn't hurt me now. I wasn't a lovesick teenager anymore. I was Sylvester-fucking Remington, highly paid right wing for the Wilcox Wombats, and I was in control.

"Call me later. Let me know if it works out."

"Okay. Thanks." I hung up, feeling better and wondering for the millionth time why I needed Rock to point out the obvious before I could get myself together. I guessed I was just glad I had him.

I rolled to pull my backpack from the floor and slipped out my laptop. I was balls deep in a data visualization course that was kicking my ass. And I'd missed a lecture tonight, only to have everything from my name to the way I ate pasta scrutinized by a five-year old.

"Shit," I moaned, scanning through the chat my group mates had been participating in for the last two hours after the lecture. We had another group project to complete, and they were basically forging ahead without me, though they'd sectioned off part of the work for me to do. Of course, since I hadn't seen the lecture yet or read the materials, I didn't have much understanding of what the assignment was or how I could contribute. Not my favorite position to be in.

I sat up, moving to the desk at the side of my room next to the window, and did my best to put the evening out of my head. I needed to buckle down and contribute, or I wouldn't pass this class. I'd already flubbed an exam thanks to a long and draining trip toward the end of the season to deliver the Seattle Krakens' butts to them on a silver platter.

ME: Sorry, getting in here late.

> JASON: No worries, Remi. Plenty of work to go around.

Yeah, I was Remi to my classmates.

They had no idea what I was up to or who I was outside of

school. It was part of the reason I'd gone with a virtual program. That, and the ongoing need for me to actually show up at practice and games. But if my classmates knew how I spent my days, I was pretty sure they'd discount my ability to pull my weight in these kinds of group projects.

I had learned from experience that people didn't tend to take me seriously in the intellectual realm. That'd been true for as long as I could remember.

ME: I'm going over the notes now.

> SARAH: Let us know if you're not sure where to get started. I've done a little data visualization at work—could jump on a call and walk you through the tools we're using.

ME: Thanks. I'll get right to it and reach out if I need anything. Sorry again for being late.

> TEIKA: Not a big deal, Remi. We all have lives too.

A little warm glow spread as I absorbed the acceptance of my classmates. I didn't want to let them down. It was no different than being with the Wombats. These guys were my team, and they depended on me. That was one thing I understood well.

I dug in, scanning the notes from the lecture and sorting through the project we'd been assigned. I was definitely going to have to do some research. I had no idea how to approach my part of the project. But luckily, it was the off-season. I had plenty of free time to research and figure it out.

I leaned back in the roller chair, turning myself to stare out the window into the darkness outside my room.

Only, it wasn't completely dark.

There was a bright square of light on the house next door.
Clara's house.

And she was standing smack in the middle of that beacon of glowing light. In a loose T-shirt and a pair of loose boxer shorts.

I had an irrational thought—were those her ex's shorts?

Then I realized these might be her pajamas, and once I pictured Clara Connor in bed, thinking was not my primary occupation.

The lights in my room were off. And I realized she probably knew that this room—the only bedroom on this side of my parents' house—was unoccupied most of the time. But since when did Clara occupy that particular window? If that'd been her room in high school, I was pretty sure I would have known about it.

I was torn. The part of me that was relishing the way she managed to be completely covered up and still look ridiculously hot wanted to keep right on watching. She was folding laundry, picking things out of a basket and then dropping them onto the foot of a bed, bending and reaching as she folded. The part of me that knew it was wrong to watch her when she had no idea I was doing it thought I really ought to go ahead and close my blinds.

Only . . .

When else did I get to just look at her, the object of pretty much all my high school fantasies? She was gorgeous in such a perfect, proper way. She'd always been the literal girl next door, and everything about her fit that role. The smooth pale skin. The generous curves sculpted in high school by youth and now firmed by what I could only guess were rigorous days in the field doing whatever she did—lassoing and pinning bears? The light-gold hair that settled around her shoulders in full waves when it was dry, and hung in sexy strands right now while it was wet.

She must've taken the master bedroom, I realized, as I had a vague memory of seeing her dad wander by that window a time or two back in school.

Clara raised a hand to her head and dropped her face into it, her posture screaming of exhaustion. And sadness.

Was she sad?

I leaned closer, wishing I could . . . what? Reach through the window and touch her? So she could recoil and tell me to get lost?

I turned away, irritated with myself. I felt like a total shitbird peeping Tom.

Finally, I stood and closed my blinds before putting myself to bed. My neighbor clearly had her own problems. I needed to keep my focus where it belonged.

But that didn't stop me from dreaming about her all night long.

I woke up frustrated and horny.

I needed a run.

CHAPTER 6

CLARA

CLOWNS. WE CAN ALL AGREE ON THOSE.

"Mommy, Siiillllvessssteeeer is running away." Katie was glued to the living room window.

"Good," I said from the dining room table where I was nursing a second cup of coffee and reviewing some of the notes from the week. The issue with being in the field all the time was that you rarely had the opportunity to take care of the office work that the field work generated. And so I ended up doing a lot of it at home. When I should have been giving Katie my full attention.

"Where is he going?" Katie turned to me and then padded across the living room to stand next to my chair, her hair a messy blond halo around her face and her pink pajamas making her look even younger than she was somehow. She looked worried. About Sly.

I sighed. "Honey, I don't know where he's going, but it doesn't matter because that isn't our business. He doesn't even really live there, so we don't need to worry about him."

She frowned. "Where does he live?"

"In Wilcox. That's where his team plays, remember?"

She grinned. "The Wombats."

"Yes." I was fighting the feeling of irritation that had come to the forefront every time I'd thought about Sly since seeing him at dinner the previous night. He had actually questioned my job choice, which really bugged me.

Maybe because I questioned it all the time too, ever since Zach had essentially brainwashed me by telling me over and over how inappropriate a job choice it was for a mother.

"Hey, Katie bear, you need to get dressed for school or we're gonna be late."

Katie's bottom lip popped out and I hoped this wasn't going to be one of those tantrum-before-school mornings. "And after school?" she asked, a hint of disapproval in her tone that suggested I'd better come up with the right answer.

"I'll be picking you up. I'm working at home today."

"Then I will work from home too." She crossed her arms and bobbed her little chin at me.

"No, you will go to school."

The lip pushed out even more. "No."

"Yep," I said, ignoring the impending tantrum on the horizon. "School first, and then we'll go to Peppi's for pizza and maybe even hit Freezy Pete's for some ice cream."

Katie didn't immediately melt down, which was a good sign. She was contemplating this deal, her head tilting to one side.

I moved while I had the advantage. "Come on, let's go find your favorite pink leggings and the dump truck top." Katie had proven herself to be a unique mix of proclivities pretty much since birth. She was definitely a girly girl—loving sparkles and rainbows and pink, but she also had some surprising favorite things—construction vehicles and skateboards, to name a couple.

"I'm tired of school," she said, but she turned to follow me to her bedroom.

"One more week after today," I reminded her, internally hoping my own plans worked out that speedily so I could be here for her more often. I was at the end of the interview process for the field supervisor position, which would put me back in the office most days, and even let me work from home more regularly.

I'd have a reliable schedule, more responsibility, and most importantly, I'd be here to take care of my daughter. There was no doubt I'd miss being in the field, but maybe it was time I make the sacrifice to care for Katie. She was worth it.

Katie sighed dramatically, but she cooperated all through getting dressed and having her hair brushed, and by the time she was finishing her toast, she was already telling me all about Celeste Adams and the birthday party she was planning for the end of June, which Katie was pretty sure would involve actual, live unicorns, and absolutely no clowns.

"We hate clowns," she said, pointing at me with her toast as if instructing me to agree.

I complied. "We do."

She nodded once, seemingly pleased that was settled.

I finally got her off to school and was just pulling back into the driveway when my phone buzzed. I glanced over at it on the passenger seat, wondering if it was work. Maybe news about the job?

I reached for the phone at the same time a loud thump came from the front of the car, and I jammed my foot onto the brake violently and screamed. Had I hit a dog? The car shuddered from a slow roll to a stop as my eyes flew to the front windshield, where Sly stood with his hands planted firmly on the hood.

Did I hit him?

Why was he shirtless? And so sweaty?

He looked angry, but I was beginning to realize maybe he was always angry when I was around.

I threw the car into park and pushed the door open and jumped out. "Are you okay? Did I hit you?"

He stood, removing his hands from my car so he could cross his arms in front of him, making the sizable muscles in his chest pop. I ripped my gaze from those and moved it back to his face.

"You don't know if you hit me?" he asked, sounding like Katie—there was clearly only one right answer here.

"I mean," I glanced back toward my phone. I still didn't know if that had been work. "I got distracted for one second. You literally came out of nowhere!"

"I literally came from the sidewalk you rammed your car over in an extremely speedy and violent fashion." He glared at me.

Wouldn't I have seen him? He must have snuck up on me somehow. "I would have seen you."

He dropped his arms and stared at me. "You clearly didn't. I can assure you, I didn't materialize out of thin air. I didn't jump out of a hedge. I was jogging. On the sidewalk."

"Hmm." I shrugged. "Okay. Sorry. I'm glad you're okay."

He shook his head. "I don't know that I am. You really startled me. I mean, you tried to kill me."

Now that it was clear he was definitely not hurt, I found myself admiring the way the sweat glistened on his tanned skin in the sunlight. His arms were like sculptures, every muscle standing out in sharp relief, every vein pulsing there beneath his skin. His torso was miles of golden skin with scattered dark hair across his chest, and all that muscle tapered down into long, loose shorts that hung across his very developed six pack. Was it an eight pack? Was that even a thing?

Shit. I was staring. "I need to get inside, so if you could move . . ."

"I don't know if I should let you get back behind the wheel. Have you been drinking today?"

"It's nine in the morning."

"So yes?"

"No!"

"Do you need me to park the car for you?"

"What?" Now I was getting pissed, and it was a welcome feeling after the irritating rush of intense attraction had threatened to humiliate me all over again. "No. Just get out of the way, please."

He stepped to the side, crossing his arms again, and making it clear that he was going to supervise me as I parked my own car in my own driveway, something I did every single day, multiple times. I glared at him and stuck my tongue out, heat rushing to my cheeks as I realized I was doing it.

Oh god, my maturity level was dropping by the second.

I pulled the car slowly into the driveway, looking both ways carefully to make sure no more hot, shirtless hockey players were going to appear out of nowhere. I turned off the engine, picked up my phone and purse, and slid back out of the car.

Sly was still standing there.

"This has been fun," I told him. "But I need to get to work." I walked around the car, heading for the back door.

"Bear wrestling on the agenda today?" he asked my back.

I spun. "What? I don't wrestle bears."

"Sounded like it last night."

"I monitor them in their habitat and sometimes rescue abandoned cubs and rehome them."

"Hm." He clearly wasn't impressed by this.

"Do you have some kind of issue with me? Or with my job?" We might as well go ahead and hash this out now. Better to do it while Katie wasn't around. She seemed to have some kind of weird fascination with the guy. Probably saw him as a potential playmate since their maturity levels were on par.

"I'm just not sure that bear wrangling is the best thing for a single mom to be spending her time with. What if something happened to you?"

Here was another guy who barely knew me, suggesting that I was making all the wrong choices for myself and for Katie. Zach had been unhappy with the person I'd turned out to be, and he'd left me on my own with a two-year old. I wasn't taking the same shit from a guy who lived next door temporarily and had zero say in what I did.

"That's really not your concern," I said, steeling my tone and my spine. "I can take care of myself and my daughter. Why don't you head on back to Wilcox so you can strap on your skates, play a game, and get overpaid some more for doing practically nothing?"

He frowned, but a flicker of something played at his expression. He looked almost . . . hurt? Offended, maybe?

"Yeah, planning to," he said, seeming to have decided that this discussion had concluded.

"Good," I said, realizing too late there was no real response needed, since he'd spun on his heel and was heading for his parents' house. Now he turned back around.

"Good," he said.

"Right."

"Good," he said again.

Well, good.

I watched his retreating form, every muscle in his back rippling in the morning sunlight, and I felt . . . what?

Shit, I felt bad.

I didn't really think professional athletes were awful. Maybe overpaid. But it was a pretty shitty thing to say to my next-door neighbor's son, especially when I depended on Violet so heavily to take care of Katie when I was at work.

I'd intended to figure out a way out of the engagement party the next day, and now I felt like I owed her again. But could I really stomach a whole evening with Sly? And a car ride in close proximity to all that . . . muscle and judgment?

It didn't matter. For right now, work was the priority. I went inside and finally checked my phone. It was a work call, but it wasn't the one I'd been hoping for. I'd already been shortlisted for the position I was vying for, but I hadn't heard anything more.

I managed to work all day without bumping into Sly again, but it became apparent after about noon that he was intent on remaining shirtless and outside all day. Not that I was stationed by the windows watching or anything.

But at one point he was out front pushing the lawnmower around wearing a backwards cap. Shirtless, of course.

Then, a bit later, he came out front with Violet, and she waved in the direction of her flower bed, which resulted in Sly appearing a few minutes later with a bucket and some gloves on, and then he proceeded to kneel down and weed the front bed. Shirtless. That took a while. Not that I was timing it.

It appeared to be pretty hot out there.

Hot, and sweaty.

And really, really sexy.

Ahem. Not that it mattered to me. At all. And honestly, was the guy even wearing sunscreen? Did he know anything about the risks of skin cancer?

At the end of the day, he was in the back with his father and Beck, waving his arms around and pointing at the falling-down fence between our backyards. I knew this because I'd decided to finish work on the covered back patio with a glass of iced tea. That old fence had been a shambles for years, and though my father had mentioned plans to fix it in the past, it never seemed like Sam was on board. And when neighbors shared a fence, I guessed they had to agree about how to fix it.

No one came to talk to me about mending fences, and I didn't get to see the conclusion of that shirtless endeavor, because I had to go pick up Katie from school, and then we spent the next couple hours at Peppi's and Freezy Pete's. By the time I was pulling very carefully back into the driveway, dusk had fallen, and the Remington house was quiet.

No shirtless hockey stars wandering about outside.

Good. That was for the best.

CHAPTER 7
SLY

WAXING AND OTHER SECRETS

I spent Friday night into the wee small hours working on my group project. Every time I'd tried to sneak upstairs to work on it, Mom and Dad had found yet another chore for me to do. I couldn't tell them why I was anxious to get up to my room, and part of me was happy to hang around outside the house in some insane and masochistic hope of bumping into Clara again.

You'd think after she practically tried to murder me with her car, I would have been wise enough to steer clear. But no one had ever accused me of being smart. In fact, just this afternoon, she'd basically asserted that I was just a dumb overpaid jock.

I mowed the lawn. I fricking pulled weeds when Mom made her most desperate pleading smile and promised me a grilled cheese sandwich when I finished. And then Dad seemed to decide that I'd only come home to do chores and mentioned some long-overdue backyard fence project, which was a whole lot more than a one-afternoon kind of gig.

Even so, by Saturday morning, I'd caught up in my classes and turned in a rough draft of my part of the project for the rest of the group to check out. I was proud of myself—it hadn't been easy. But I'd buckled down and gotten the thing done.

I had a bachelor's already, but it wasn't like I'd really earned it myself. There'd been help at every turn when I was in college, with everyone in my life right there to make sure I didn't miss a game, never took my eye off the all-important puck.

I mean, I love the game, don't get me wrong.

But sometimes it felt like everyone else only loved me for the game. If that made any sense.

"Sylvester, come out here please," Mom was calling from the kitchen. I'd just gotten back from my run, had managed to avoid being almost mowed down in Clara's driveway, and was not feeling my freshest, but I didn't like to keep Mom waiting.

"What's up, Ma?" I asked, stepping into the kitchen, which smelled delicious. "Ooh, bacon."

"Help yourself," she said, smiling. "Now. Have you given any thought to what you'll wear tonight?"

"What? No. Not really. I mean . . . a shirt, for sure."

Mom made her don't-be-an-idiot face. "You'll need to look nice."

"So I should shower?"

Now she rolled her eyes.

"I just don't want you to give Clara the wrong idea." She wrung her hands in front of her and looked concerned about me giving my neighbor, who definitely hated me, an idea that would not be right.

"What would the right idea be? Just so I can compare."

Mom lifted an eyebrow as I took a third piece of bacon and leaned against the counter. "The right idea would be something like, 'that Sylvester is very handsome and polite, and perhaps I would enjoy getting to know him a little better.'" Mom delivered this in a high-pitched voice I assumed was meant to be Clara's, and then she wiggled her eyebrows suggestively.

I frowned down at her. "You're setting me up with Clara? That's what this is? And you are encouraging me to . . ." I wiggled my eyebrows back. This was a bad idea.

Mom sighed and slouched. "Oh Sylvester, I just hate seeing

you alone . . . and poor Clara over there, losing both her parents so fast, and that awful man running out on her and Katie . . .”

“Running out?” I asked, my blood starting to heat in misplaced anger.

“Well, I mean, I don’t know the whole story. But he’s not around, and she won’t talk about him.”

“Good.”

Ma squinted at me. “What?”

“Nothing. No, not good. I just mean, he sounds like a turd.” I was glad he wasn’t around. But was that selfish? Wouldn’t it be better for Katie to have her dad?

“Language.” Mom swatted my arm.

“Ouch. That’s not even a bad word, Ma.”

“So I’m saying you dress up nicely and you show her a good time.”

“That’s what I’m known for.” More eyebrow wiggling.

Mom hit me again, harder.

“Ow.”

I took three more pieces of bacon off the platter as Mom busied herself around the kitchen, and just as I was about to head back upstairs, she stopped me. “Sly?”

“Yeah?”

“You were a big help today.”

“It’s no problem.”

“I was just wondering . . . you have a couple months off, don’t you?”

I turned slowly to look at my mother, who was wearing the expression that had convinced me to do one million chores today. “Yeah,” I answered, my voice wary.

“Well, wouldn’t it be nice if you could spend them here? With us?”

“Here?”

“Yes. At home.”

I looked around the place I’d grown up suddenly considering it very differently. Not as my parents’ house that I visited once in a blue moon. But as a place I'd once lived. Could I live here again? Even for a couple months? "Ummm," I drew the word out as thoughts of school flicked through my mind. This summer was supposed to be about school.

"We could even clean out that little apartment over the garage for you. I know you're too big to want to sleep in your old bedroom." Mom dropped my gaze, wringing her hands in front of her. "It might just be nice, with your dad slowing down, you know . . ."

"Is Dad okay?" Little pricks of my constant worry about Dad's health flared into full-blown concern.

"He is, yes, of course he is. He's just older, and I don't think that fence is something he can do alone. And the boxes in the garage, and . . . it would just be nice to have you around."

"Sure, Mom," I said, even though staying here all summer had definitely not been part of the plan.

She stepped close and leaned up on her toes to kiss my cheek as she patted my arm. "Really? That's wonderful. Thank you, honey."

I felt a little sideswiped as I stepped away from her, but a tiny bloom of excitement spread through me too. Clara and I would be neighbors again. For the summer.

I headed back upstairs to finish reading a scintillating book about analytic techniques in the age of artificial intelligence, and told myself I would not be thinking about Clara and whether she was sad.

I didn't like thinking of her sad.

Then again, I didn't like thinking of her all snobby and smart like she usually was, either.

My mind automatically reverted to thinking about her in other ways. More physical ways. Which actually made it very difficult to study.

I glanced at the door, making sure it was locked, and put the book aside, stretching out on my bed and slipping one hand down my shorts as I folded the other arm back behind my head and let my eyes slide shut.

Thinking about Clara at all had an effect on me, and it was getting harder to ignore.

I fisted myself roughly, recalling the way she'd looked when she'd first stepped into Mom's house Thursday night, the way her golden hair had fallen down over her delicate collarbone, and how those pouty lips of hers had been painted dark.

What would those lips look like wrapped around me? I pumped harder now, imagining it. Fuck, she was hot. I considered what a good girl she'd always been and wondered what that would be like in the bedroom. As I jerked myself off, I imagined her in my room, leaning forward over my bed with her dress flipped up to reveal that perfect peach of an ass. God, what I wouldn't give to stand behind her, see her looking over her pale shoulder at me with that teasing glint in her deep ocean eyes. What I wouldn't do to feel myself sliding inside her, gripping the flesh at her hips and making her scream my name.

That did it. The thought of turning the good girl bad had me spurting over my stomach, and almost immediately feeling a surge of guilt about using her that way, for my own gratification. The guilt was not terribly deep, however. Mostly I felt good. And ready to face her for the engagement party.

I'd shower and dress nicely, as Mom had asked. And then I'd be the perfect gentleman. Clara wouldn't know what hit her. She'd find herself uncontrollably attracted to me, unable to resist the charms that had won over so many women before her. And then maybe, just maybe, I'd fuck her and finally get the girl out of my system.

But I already knew two things for sure. One, there was no way I'd just charm and fuck a woman like Clara. She was too smart, too classy, and too good for that. And two, if she'd been in my system this long, the odds of fucking her out in one night were slim to none. Clara was a problem I had for good, no matter what else my life held. Some part of me would always have it bad for the smart girl next door.

"Sylvester, are you ready?" Mom's voice came through the door, pulling me out of a very deep sleep.

Shit. I was asleep? I definitely hadn't planned to fall asleep . . . but I'd been all drowsy after my afternoon slapstick session, and then I'd let myself doze. I looked at my watch. And now it was fifteen after five?

"Uh, yeah, one minute," I yelled through the door.

"Clara is expecting you soon," she called, sending my adrenaline spiking even more. I needed a shower, and I'd planned to take my time getting dressed and arriving at Clara's cool, calm, and collected. Instead I was going to be sweaty, stressed, and whatever the opposite of collected was.

"Yeah, I know, I'll—" I pulled open the door, planning to sneak to the bathroom before Mom realized I hadn't showered, but she was still standing right outside the door. "Oh. Wow, you look great, Mom."

"Don't flatter me. You haven't even showered!"

"But you really do look amazing. That dress makes your eyes pop."

Mom's mad face slid just an inch. "You're going to be late." Some of the anger had left her voice.

"Don't worry about me. You and Dad go on ahead, and I'll be right behind you."

"With Clara and Katie."

"With Clara and Katie," I repeated. "And they will be charmed and impressed by my gentlemanly wiles and excellent fashion sense."

Mom pressed her lips into a line like she didn't agree with any of this, but then she seemed to realize that time was wasting. I dashed past her into the bathroom.

Ten minutes later, I was locking the front door and heading next door, only about seven minutes behind schedule, and looking pretty fucking good, if I did say so myself. I'd put on my black slacks and a tie, and I had a tailored sport coat in case Mom insisted I needed a jacket.

I rang the doorbell at Clara's and waited, feeling a surprising twitch of nerves battling in my gut. I hadn't been nervous around a woman in . . . well, since high school. Maybe I wasn't nervous now. Maybe it was all the bacon.

The door opened a couple inches, but Clara didn't appear in the crack, and then the door slammed shut again.

What the hell?

I was about to ring the doorbell again, when the door opened once more, and this time, I looked a lot farther down than I had the first time and caught a tiny blond head and a sparkling blue eye before the door slammed shut again.

"This must be one of those magic re-closing doors," I said loudly, sinking to my knees to catch the little imp at eye level next time. "I've heard about these, but thought they were only installed at very fancy palaces or—"

The door opened again, only this time, it opened all the way, and I found myself staring at a pair of very sexy tanned legs that ended in navy blue strappy sandals.

"What in the world?" Clara asked, sounding already exasperated with me.

I stood, brushing off my slacks, and shot the tiny person at her side a quick squint. There would be retribution later. She'd made me look like an idiot. Again.

"Ah, yeah. Sorry, dropped my keys." I held up the keys and took my first full look at Clara's face, and then nearly dropped them for real. "Wow. You look. I mean. Wow."

She frowned at me. "Okay."

"He thinks you look pretty, Mommy," Katie said, earning back a bit of my trust. "What about me?" she stepped past her mother and did a twirl on the porch, sending her purple skirt into a swirl around her. She wore some kind of toy tractor on a string around her neck, which seemed like an odd choice of jewelry, but I wasn't about to challenge Katie. I already knew she'd probably win.

"You both look really beautiful," I said, looking at Katie because seeing Clara's deep eyes framed with smoky makeup and her mouth painted in that devilish shade of dark red made me question my ability to speak.

"You clean up pretty well too," Clara said. "I see you found a shirt."

What did that mean? "I have several shirts," I told her, not sure whether I was going to be offended about whatever she was getting at.

"Who knew?" she said breezily, stepping up to lock the front door and then heading down the steps ahead of me.

Katie and I exchanged puzzled glances and then we all headed to my car. As I helped Clara into the passenger seat, I was glad I'd decided to bring the sedan instead of the truck. Katie settled into the seat Mom had shoved into my car this morning as I walked around to slide into the driver's side, and soon, Clara's scent filled the car as we moved toward the restaurant and I struggled to find words.

Half Full wasn't a big town, but it did have a developed downtown area that drew people from most of the neighboring areas, thanks to a variety of bars, restaurants, and even a new club.

"Good weekend?" I asked Clara, hoping to start us off on a very civil foot for the evening.

"So far, so good," she said, giving me very little to work with. "You?"

"Yeah. Nice to be back. And I managed to get some homework handled, so—" Shit. Why did I tell her that? I'd told literally no one that I was back in school.

"Homework?"

"I, uh . . ." memories swamped me then, of Clara at our kitchen table watching me battle algebra problems with no luck at all. Watching me practically melt down with the effort. Watching me reveal the truth I'd been hiding since then—that I had very little working for me upstairs. "It's not a big deal. Forget I said anything. What have you been up to?"

She was quiet just a beat too long, and then Katie piped up. "I hate homework. Homework is for chumps and losers."

Clara turned around in her seat. "Who told you that?"

"Curt Andrews."

"Well, Curt Andrews is a chump and a loser if he thinks that," I suggested.

"Curt Andrews is six," Clara told me, sounding disappointed in me for maligning a child.

"Homework is important," I tried again, suddenly desperate for Clara not to be mad at me. At least not yet.

"Sly is right," Clara said, lighting a little glow in my chest. "Doing the work now sets you up for the future. Even Sly was doing homework this weekend." I hated that little "even" she threw in there. Like I was a cautionary tale.

"Mom worked from home yesterday and then today we got manicures and Mom got parts of herself waxed that we don't talk about." Katie whispered this last part and I worked to maintain a neutral expression. Clara getting things waxed was something I was finding it hard to think about without certain parts of my body trying to get involved in the consideration.

Clara sighed. "So, Katie. When I said we didn't talk about it, I meant, like right now. With other people."

"It's only Siiiillllllvesssssterrrr."

I shot a smile at Clara, but she didn't return it.

So much for gentlemanly small talk. And since I was driving, getting blazingly drunk wasn't an option. This was going to be a long evening.

Actually, it was going to be a long summer.

CHAPTER 8
CLARA

THINKING IS FRAUGHT WITH PERIL

This had the potential to be a very long night.

For one thing, Sly looked ridiculously hot in his fitted black pants and tie. I wasn't sure I'd ever seen him dressed up, except the night I'd watched him through the front windows of my house as he'd helped Suzie Barkin into a limo and then climbed in behind her for his senior prom. He'd been wearing a tux, and the image still showed up in some of my less-guarded moments.

He was so handsome.

And he so clearly knew it.

The thing was . . . there had always been something about Sly Remington, something that never really revealed itself but that I'd glimpsed here and there. It was almost like beneath all the hot guy accessories—the hair, the smile, the body, the hockey stardom—he was trying to hide that he was more normal than anyone suspected. It was like the opposite of Clark Kent and his Superman alter ego. Sly was the superhero all the time, and he didn't want anyone to know there was a decent guy lurking behind the Wombat jersey.

But maybe I was wrong.

I'd seen shots of him at his hockey games looking cocky and mean, shots of him making out with women around Wilcox or after games when the team traveled. Maybe that was the real Sly Remington.

Sly parked and we headed inside the hotel where the engagement party was being held at the fancy restaurant within. I noticed a few people watching us as we walked in, and I realized that they might recognize Sly. They probably did—hometown hero and all. And I wondered who they thought I was. His latest fling? But then there was Katie . . .

There wasn't much more time to think about the weird homework statement he'd made—did hockey players actually study the game in their free time?—or the fact that Katie had mentioned my waxing . . .

Beck greeted us at the entrance and from that point forward, I was included with the family as we were introduced to Zara's family. There was so much enthusiastic talk and champagne being passed around, I did my best to smile and say hello when appropriate.

Katie was immediately adopted by the other kids who were already at the restaurant, which the party had taken over entirely. They were poking around the DJ up at the front of the room and taking turns running across the dance floor.

I excused myself after a little while to check in with Katie and then head to the restroom, if only to get a break from the chaos of the party. I was just touching up my lipstick when Zara emerged from a stall.

"You look incredible tonight," she said, beaming at me in the mirror. Zara had a wide friendly smile with full lips, and the emerald green sheath she wore showed off her curves and lit up her sharp blue eyes.

"So do you. Congratulations. Officially, I mean."

Her smile widened. "Thanks so much. I'm still just floored that this is my life. That this guy chose me, you know?"

I did know. I'd felt that way once. But it had fallen apart so quickly and so completely that I didn't have anything to say to the sentiment. I nodded.

"So . . . you and Sly?" she grinned at me and I waited for the rest of the question, but it didn't come.

"We went to high school together. He was older."

"Right, Beck told me that. And that you used to tutor him."

I dropped her eyes and put my lipstick back in my purse. "Ah, yeah. For a little while."

"And now?"

I looked up again, wondering if she really thought there was something going on with us. "Now he's in town for the weekend. I'm a little worried his mother thinks we're destined to be together since we're both single."

"Oh yeah? Violet means well though, I'm sure. And you wouldn't be interested in having there be anything else between you?"

"I mean . . . he doesn't live here. He's famous. I'm honestly just trying to make Violet happy."

"That's it, huh?" she winked.

"It is."

"Anyway, I guess I'd better get back out there!" Zara gave me one last huge smile and left the room.

I stood for a few more minutes staring at myself in the mirror.

I cleared my throat, rolled my shoulders back and gave myself a stern look in the mirror before heading back outside to rejoin the party. There was nothing going on here with Sly. And there never would be.

Katie and the other kids were dancing out on the parquet floor in the center of the room, and she gave me a happy grin as I walked by. At least one of us was having a great time.

"Champagne?" A server paused at my side with a tray full of crystal flutes full of sparkling golden champagne.

"Thank you." I took one, and took a long sip, and then my eyes found Sly. He was standing with his back to me, talking with Beck and some other men I didn't recognize. I moved to the table where my name was placed before a plate in a beautiful gold script, and sat down. My eyes were drawn back across the room to that wide muscular back, the dark hair in lush sexy waves on his head. He wore it longer than he had in high school. It had a kind of unkempt perfection that I liked, as if it was just waiting for someone to run her hands through it. I could imagine Sly laughing as she did it, that sexy rumble of mirth coming from deep inside his chest, his dark eyes sparkling.

How many women had gotten to see that first hand?

Why did I care?

I forced myself to turn around, toying with my name tag as I finished the champagne. I didn't care. My life was good. Complete. I had Katie, and she was healthy and happy, even without her dad around. And I had fantastic and supportive neighbors and friends, and my own house that I owned outright, thanks to my parents. And I had a job that was challenging and exciting. Of course I was halfheartedly hoping to change that last part so I could be a better mom to Katie.

"I always worried you were going to hurt yourself someday, doing something just like this." Sly's deep rumble came from over my shoulder, and he sat in the chair at my side, placing another flute of champagne in front of me.

"Sitting at a table? I'm not that clumsy," I assured him, already feeling my ire pricking up for yet another fight.

"Nah. Thinking too hard." His smile was easy, light. He didn't have that air about him that told me he was trying to get to me.

I relaxed a tad and wished I had more champagne. "I was just enjoying the party," I lied.

"And thinking."

"Maybe a little."

"Want to play twenty questions?"

I raised an eyebrow.

"I'll guess what you were thinking about."

"Okay," I said. He didn't have a big enough ego to guess that I'd been thinking about how sexy he was, did he?

"Were you thinking about Katie?"

"I mean, that's not fair. I'm a mom. I'm always thinking about her somehow. Maybe not actively."

"So one point for me."

"You don't keep points in twenty questions."

"Maybe you've been playing wrong." Sly's big body was relaxed at my side, and his face kept that easy smile. What would it be like to get to be the woman at his side all the time? To have that smile warming the space around me? To know that when it was all over, we'd be leaving together?

"Half a point."

"Fine. Were you thinking about work?"

"A little bit."

"Another point."

"Half point." Though maybe that one deserved a full point.

"How many things can you think about at one time?"

I laughed. "A woman's mind is a deep and complicated place, Sly. I can think about lots of things at once."

"Were you thinking about me in there at all?" His easy smile dropped, and a little line appeared between his brows.

My stomach flipped. I couldn't possibly tell him I was. "You?"

He lifted one shoulder and gazed at me with a vulnerable expression I'd never seen on his face before. And then he said, "If I were to be honest, I might let it slip that I've been thinking about you. A lot."

It was like someone had upended a bottle of glitter inside me, spilled it down my spine. But I tried not to react. It didn't matter. I didn't want to be another girl on Sly Remington's list. I couldn't be. I had responsibilities. "I, uh . . ." What the hell was I supposed to say to that? "I was probably thinking about you a little bit. In there with all the other stuff."

He leaned in closer and I could see the very beginning of a shadow starting along his jaw, smell that leathery sexy scent he wore. Or was that just him? My brain was starting to scramble with proximity.

Oh god. He was staring at my lips. "Really? You were, huh?"

The entire room had tunneled down to this one table, this tiny space in which just the two of us sat. I didn't hear the music, the noise of conversation. I heard only my heart, beating loud and hopeful.

I had no idea what to say, how to respond. I felt myself drawn to him, leaning in, but I knew I couldn't kiss him here, in the middle of this party, with Katie nearby. Or at all. I screwed my eyes shut and forced myself back, turning toward the table and waving to a passing waiter for another glass of champagne.

"I was thinking how great you are with Katie." I took a long swallow of champagne as I felt the charged tension between us begin to recede and the room opened up again. My eyes found my daughter, laughing with another little girl at a table across the room.

"Katie is great," he said. "Clever and fun. You're a really great mother."

It felt so good to hear someone say it, but he didn't know that. He'd been around for a whole three days. "I'm gone all the time."

"I think you're there when it counts."

"Your mother probably spends more time with her than I do."

"Kids need lots of role models, Clara. There's nothing wrong with that. My mom is a great influence. Katie will learn which fork to use when and how to mix cocktails in crazy colors. Super important."

I chuckled at that and risked a glance at Sly's face, surprised to see it full of compassion, the eyes warm and wide. "Your mom is great. And Katie loves her. I just need to figure out how to be there for her more regularly as she gets older, starts to encounter real issues and questions."

He nodded. "Yeah, maybe. You got a plan?"

I sighed. "I'm on the short list for a supervisory position. Regular hours, in the office and remote."

"No more wrestling bears?" He lifted half his mouth in a sexy little smile and a warm shiver went through me. I took another sip of champagne.

"Sly, I don't wrestle bears. I help track them, occasionally sedate them so we can tag them or place an orphan cub with a particular mama bear, and I study their habitat and behaviors."

"Tomato, potato," he said with a shrug. "Won't you miss it? Sounds like you like it."

"Yeah." I tried not to think about that. The natural light replaced with the fluorescent bulbs of the office, the sound of birds and wind and rushing water supplanted by the noise of telephone calls and printers whirring. "But I'll adjust. It's better for Katie. And I haven't gotten the job anyway." I could barely admit to myself that part of me hoped I wouldn't get it.

"Maybe not yet. But you will. You're the kind of woman who gets what she sets out to get." He said this with such confidence I found myself staring at him, forgetting myself.

"I am?"

"Hell yes. It's what makes you so fucking sexy. That determination, that confidence. I wish I had half of it."

"You're a friggin' hockey star. I'm sure you've got plenty of drive."

He shrugged, the open smile dropping. "I'm not sure it's drive. It might just be a different kind of determination."

I shook my head. "What do you mean?"

"If I didn't play hockey, what the hell would I do?" he asked. Before I could offer an answer, he added. "You saw first hand that I'm not the sharpest tool in the box. I was just lucky I could skate, or who knows where I'd be."

I might have gaped. The sexy and successful winger for the Wilcox Wombats was full of self doubt? I'd never seen Sly Remington as anything but cocky and ready to take on the world.

"I don't think that's true," I said. "There's a difference between being intelligent and being great at algebra."

"They're definitely connected."

I thought back to those long evenings at his kitchen table, the books between us. "It's possible your tutor wasn't as focused as she could have been."

He frowned. "My lack of brainpower is definitely not on you."

I wondered, though. I was so busy wishing for things that could never happen back then that I might have let him down. I didn't want to go there. "You mentioned homework earlier. What did you mean?"

Sly dropped my eyes, his big hand toying with the knife at his place setting. He pressed his lips together and gave me a quick look. "Can I tell you a secret?"

"Sure."

"Seriously. No one knows."

"Okay." What was he going to say? I braced myself.

"I'm working on my MBA."

Surprise rippled through me, but I tried not to let it show. "That's amazing."

"It'll be amazing if I actually get it."

"That's not what I meant at all. Of course you'll get it, if you want it. What will you do with it?"

He leaned back in the chair, sighed. "Not sure yet. But I know I can't skate forever. I need a backup plan."

"That's really smart." I had assumed he'd play as long as he could and then live off the money. I admired that he wanted to do something else.

"We'll see. I'd appreciate it if you didn't mention it to my family. I'd rather not have anyone else be let down if I fail."

He looked defeated, something I hadn't seen since those evenings at the kitchen table. "You won't fail," I told him, dropping a hand on his forearm and almost immediately wishing I hadn't. His arm was warm and so very solid and alive. Masculine. Heat rushed through me at the contact.

"That's nice of you, Clara. School, historically, is not my strength, though." His words were soft, and he delivered them staring directly into my eyes, reconnecting the thread I'd felt pulling us closer since I'd run into him again on Violet's doorstep that day. As I stared into those dark eyes, my hand on his thick forearm, something clicked inside me, some inevitability. I could already see us together. And just beyond that vision, I could see another. Me. Heartbroken and alone.

Because Sly Remington was not made for me. I'd learned that a long time ago.

"Mom!" Katie appeared at my other side, breaking the tension I'd fallen victim to. I pulled my hand back and turned away from Sly, relief washing through me. Why did I want something so badly when I already knew how much it would hurt?

"Hey Katie bear. Are you having fun?" My daughter's cheeks were flushed pink and the ribbon in her hair had disappeared.

"So much fun," she gushed. "But I'm so thirsty. And they said it's time for the dinner." She reached for the goblet of water in front of her and gulped it enthusiastically.

Soon, I traded the searing tension of the conversation with Sly for the careful oversight of helping a five-year old doing her best to negotiate her way out of vegetables by trading single bites for privileges like some kind of hostage rescue advisor.

"If I eat another bite of broccoli, I get two pieces of cake."

"I don't think so," I told her.

"Sillllvessssster?"

I stiffened, looking between them. "Why are you asking him? He's not in charge here."

Sly chuckled at this and leaned forward. "Your mom's in charge, Katie. Definitely." His eyes found mine for a beat and something hot and needy slid through me.

Heat pooled between my legs and I swallowed down the sudden desire I felt.

"Eat your vegetables and maybe your mom will say yes to the other thing we talked about."

Sly and Katie had been negotiating behind my back? I found my words. "What other thing?"

"Sillllveeessssster is going to teach me to skate," Katie practically yelled around a mouthful of broccoli.

Sly was quickly winding his way into our lives, and I was beginning to realize that right now was the time to stop it if I wanted to.

The thing was, I was realizing I didn't really want to.

CHAPTER 9
SLY

STANDING ON ONE FOOT

I was happy for my brother and Zara, of course. It was a beautiful party, and they really looked like a great fit—totally in love, ready to plunge into a future together. And I wasn't unhappy for me, either.

I'd spent the whole meal by Clara's side, and every now and then I indulged in a little fantasy that we were on a real date. That I'd finally get the girl at the end of the night.

But Katie was right there.

It was hard to sit through dinner. It was also hard making polite conversation with those around us, realizing that with every word I was more assured at Clara's kindness, her intelligence, and her self-assurance. She was beautiful and wise, and such a good mother. It was hard admitting that my mother had been right. This was the kind of woman I wanted.

Actually, this was the woman I wanted. But could a woman like Clara actually be interested in a guy like me? Had anything changed since I was the jock with the impossible crush on the good girl? And beyond that, I was in the middle of something. Something important. Clara, while a beautiful and welcome distraction, would still be a distraction.

We made polite conversation with those around us, and I did my best to put on the charm for these folks at the table we'd just met, who turned out to be good friends of Zara's parents back in Richmond. But my mind was not in the game. It was very much focused on the increasing desire I felt for Clara, and on the subtle hints I thought I was picking up that she might feel the same way. Shared glances, a brush of her fingers on my arm as she reached for her water.

Katie was a good tension breaker. Every now and then, she'd share a random fact with me out of the blue and usually around a mouthful of rice or salmon.

"I can stand on one foot longer than any of my friends."

"I read at a third grade level, did you know that?"

"My friend Toby has a pet dragon. It's super small. Like a little dinosaur. Its name is Hamlet."

The longer we sat at that table, the party going on around us in the form of laughter, soft music, and tinkling silverware, the more I learned about Katie, and the more I wanted to know particular things about Clara.

Did she like a light touch or something more assertive?

Did she let out sexy little sounds when she was turned on?

Did her hands explore when she was being touched, loved, or did she stay still, gripping the sheets and just feeling?

I shouldn't care, but I was done acting like I wasn't going to let things progress just as far as Clara was willing to take them. I'd waited my whole life for this chance. Or that's what it felt like, at least.

"I had a really good time," Katie told me when we were back in the car, heading home. Her little face was right in the center of the back seat when I glanced in the mirror, but her presence filled the whole car, jovial and sweet, full of excitement after a big night out. It was hard to resent her presence.

"I'm glad. I hope your mom had a good time too," I said, my voice dropping though I didn't plan for it to.

The dark streets slid by on either side of my car, lights like watercolor streaks against the deep grey of a summer night. I risked a glance at Clara.

"I did," she said quietly, and for a minute I worried that the studious girl had gone back into her safe space, that she was using the quiet and the dark to analyze the new awareness between us, to decide if it was right or wrong.

I was afraid what she'd decide.

But then her hand crept quietly across the center console, finding my shoulder and squeezing gently before returning to her own side of the car. Sudden warmth poured through me. That tiny touch seemed to promise so much more.

Or it could have been just a friendly gesture. But no, there was something here, wasn't there? Why was I so uncertain? Things were never this complex with the women I usually dated.

I pulled up in front of Clara's house and turned the car off, which brought the dome lights up. Somewhere along the way, exuberant Katie had drifted off to sleep, but the alteration of motion had snapped her back awake.

"We're home?" she asked, groggy.

"Yep, let's get you to bed," Clara suggested.

Even though I felt a sadness anticipating the loss of their company, of course Clara was right.

"I'm not sleepy," Katie announced loudly.

Clara unsnapped Katie's booster harness and I scooped the kid up and put her on my shoulders for the walk to the door. She cackled with glee and whooped.

"Careful," Clara said.

"He won't hurt me," Katie assured her.

"I was more worried about Sly," Clara said, meeting my eyes. "He doesn't want to get hurt doing silly things, then he won't be able to play hockey."

"Speaking of hockey," I said, craning my neck to see Katie above me as we reached the front door. "Would you guys have time tomorrow afternoon to meet at the rink in town? I could give you your first lesson, Katie."

A squeal answered me from above, but it was Clara I was waiting for. She unlocked the front door, pulling it open and switching on the lights inside, and then reached for Katie, pulling her off my shoulders as I ducked my head.

"Can we, Mommy? Silllvesssterrr is gonna teach me to skate!"

Clara put Katie down and smiled at her. "Yeah, I suppose we could."

My feet were suddenly lighter. "I'll be there pretty often this week. We've got an exhibition game in Wilcox three weeks out," I explained.

Clara was staring up at me, an expression on her face I couldn't quite read. "What time?"

"Around two? Or three? Whenever you can."

She nodded. "Do we need skates?"

"We can borrow some there if you don't have your own."

A soft smile lit her face. "We don't."

Just then, headlights flashed across where we stood on the doorstep as Mom and Dad pulled in next door.

Any hopes I was harboring that there'd be a good night kiss or anything else were slowly fading. Clara had Katie to worry about, and Mom was hustling across Clara's grass in our direction.

"Did you kids have a nice night?" Mom called.

"Yes!" Katie confirmed loudly.

"She's all hopped up on chocolate cake and sparkling cider," I told Mom.

"Glad to hear it," Mom said. "Clara, I'm so glad you both could join us. Please do save the date for the wedding, too. The actual save the dates will be out this week, but it's August thirtieth. And did you hear that Sly will be staying with us all summer? So you two can attend together."

I stuffed down a groan. Mom had stolen my thunder.

"I didn't hear that," Clara said, her eyes finding my face and narrowing slightly as if trying to figure out why I hadn't mentioned it. "That's great." I wasn't sure she believed the words.

Had I misread things? "Thank you so much for including us, Violet. We'd better get this one off to bed!"

And just like that, the night was over, leaving me full of anticipation pinging around inside me. It wasn't far off from the way I'd felt in high school when a tenth-grade Clara would come over twice a week to help me work on math, which had also been Mom's idea.

I wrapped an arm around my mother's shoulders as we crossed the lawn and headed home. Maybe Mom had known something all those years ago that I hadn't.

When we got inside, Dad had already gone to bed, and I followed Mom to the kitchen, where she put on a kettle for tea.

"I'm so glad you're here, honey," she told me, setting two mugs out on the counter and dropping bags into them.

"Me too, Mom." It was a little close, being back at my parents' place, but it was nice being home again.

"You and Clara are getting along well," she said, as if this was just an innocent observation.

"You can stop," I told her. "Whatever's going to happen there will happen. It's complicated."

She raised an eyebrow and poured hot water into the mugs, then came to the table after placing sugar and milk in the center. She slid a steaming mug to me. "What do you mean, 'complicated'?"

"She has a kid, for starters." Weirdly, this wasn't the deal breaker I'd always thought it would be.

"Do you like her?"

"I'm not twelve, Mom."

"Do you like her, Sly? Like you did in high school?" Mom was watching me closely, and I knew she already saw much more than I'd told her. Moms had that scary kid-perception ability. Like how she'd always known when I was lying as a kid, even though I was an excellent liar.

"Yeah," I said, trying not to give too much away. "I mean, of course. She's gorgeous."

"And?"

I stared at Mom and then dropped my eyes to my tea. "Let's just leave it at that for now, okay?"

I could feel my mother's eyes on me for a beat more, and then she sighed and leaned back in her chair. "I just want to see both my boys happy."

"I'm happy already, and it has nothing to do with your neighbor." Of course even I was starting to think I could be even happier with her neighbor.

"I'm glad."

And I was glad that Mom was willing to accept that answer and that we weren't going to do a deep dive into my mental state to look at all the ways hockey wouldn't keep me warm at night. That's what the team psych was for, anyway.

"Hey, Mom?"

Mom's eyes lifted in question and she made a little noise.

"Can we start cleaning out the apartment over the garage tomorrow?"

Mom sighed, passing a hand across her forehead. "I told you we would, but I don't know if I'm up to clearing all that out," she said. "Which is why it's still shoved in there." A lot of what was stored up there had gotten shoved into the little apartment when Mom's dad passed, leaving her with a house to empty and too many decisions to be made. I suspected she'd compensated by simply moving most of his things to the apartment and ignoring them.

"I could help with that."

My mother held my gaze for a long beat, and I could see the emotions flickering through her light blue eyes. Finally, she nodded. "That would be a big help, actually. I've just had such a hard time getting myself to go up there at all. It's too much."

"I know, Mom." A flash of precognition hit me – what would it be like when my own parents were gone? What must it be like for Clara?

"But it makes sense. If you're going to stay all summer, you shouldn't have to sleep in your childhood bedroom, no matter how much I enjoy knowing you're in there."

I smiled at the woman who'd always looked out for me, who I knew would always see me as a little boy in some ways.

"Thanks." I'd get to work on that the next day. The idea of having a private place was nice, but I wasn't going to pretend that I wasn't also considering the possibility of getting Clara alone somewhere at some point, and with Katie and my parents around, that was a bit more complicated than I'd have liked.

Sunday morning was busy. I'd already pulled half the boxes from the apartment down to the garage by noon, and was beginning to sort things into piles to donate and keep. Of course Mom was going to be the final say, but I knew that she was immobilized by the decisions, so if she just wanted me to handle it, I would.

The apartment was dusty and had that unlived in, unloved feeling without all the boxes and extra furniture shoved into haphazard piles across its little living room. The place wasn't big —just a bedroom and then a kind of all-purpose space that consisted of the living room, a little eating space in the bay window that looked out over the driveway, and a kitchenette to one side. There was a bathroom with a decent-sized shower too.

It would work, I thought with satisfaction. I'd just need to upgrade the bed if I wanted to get any decent sleep through the off-season. If my parents wanted to use this as a guest space, I'd make it as nice as I could. I could imagine Beck and Zara staying here someday, maybe with a crib in the corner. Strangely, for the first time, I considered that maybe one day I'd be the one with a family, but as soon as I had the thought, I put it away. The immediate need was an air conditioning unit. It was swampy up there, and the old window unit was on its last legs.

By noon, I was headed into town. I ran my errands for the apartment and ended up at the rink with a half-hour to spare before Katie and Clara showed up.

I'd called Arnold Leighton, the guy who ran the place and had since I'd been in high school, and he was happy to meet me there and set us up for a few hours. I'd mentioned to him that I was staying a while and he'd offered to let me get on the ice in the early afternoons before the summer leagues practiced.

I usually made a point of staying off skates for at least a full month when the season was over, but now I was itching to feel the speed and freedom that came with moving across the ice. It was in my blood, and when there weren't six guys in pads waiting to knock me off my feet, skating was pure fun.

CHAPTER 10
CLARA

PINK IS THE FASTEST COLOR

I didn't sleep well. I had strange misplaced ideas about Sly and the way he'd watched me and attended to my daughter all through dinner. And the new revelation that he'd be next door all summer wasn't finding an easy place to settle.

I knew I shouldn't entertain the kinds of feelings and ideas that were starting to fly around inside me.

Still, the way he'd looked at me was hard to forget.

He'd looked at me like he might actually be thinking the same kinds of things about me. I told myself it was unlikely.

But that was my teenaged heartbreak talking, mostly. I was having trouble separating the grown woman I was from the insecure girl I'd been.

The problem?

We both found Sly Remington way too hot.

The other obvious issue was Katie. Sly and I had no better chance of finding time alone together than we might have had in high school, had he shown the slightest bit of interest then. Between houses full of other people and unrelenting schedules, it wasn't like we were going to suddenly find ourselves alone together. In a room with a bed.

And dammit, I really needed to drag my mind out of the gutter. Or out of Sly Remington's pants, at least.

These were the thoughts flying through my mind as I drove Katie to the ice rink in Boomsmack, the next town over. Half Full didn't have an ice rink, but once Sly mentioned it, I did remember spending a few days skating as a kid over at the rink in Boomsmack.

"Maybe I'll be a pro ice hockey player like Sillllvester." Katie had been talking nonstop since we got into the car. She had on gloves and a knit cap even though I'd suggested that she wait to put them on until we were in the rink.

"You can be anything you want, Katie bear," I told her, hoping one day it would actually be true. Maybe by the time she was an adult the world would be as much action as it was talk about equality, though I kind of hoped that wouldn't mean Katie actually playing hockey. I couldn't stand watching her get hit all the time.

We pulled up and a few minutes later, we were ducking through the front doors and into the quiet coolness of the rink's lobby. I'd expected kids everywhere and some general form of chaos, but it was almost silent inside.

"Hello." A man stood from where he'd been sitting next to the empty ticket window. "I'm Arnold. Sly said you'd be needing some skates."

I glanced around, still expecting to see other people somewhere, but it was pretty clear we were the only ones here. "Slow day at the ice rink," I said, smiling at the man.

"Oh, not usually. Sly rented the place out for a few hours." Arnold led us to the side of the rink and I got my first view of the ice. It was smooth and empty, gleaming under the overhead lights. I figured when you were a pro hockey player, you could afford to rent out a whole rink to practice. Maybe. It seemed excessive, though, and Sly didn't strike me as that kind of guy. "Sizes?" Arnold asked, interrupting my confusion.

"She's a kids' twelve," I told him.

"And you?"

"Oh no, I'm not skating."

"Just in case?"

"I don't think so—"

"Mom!" Katie was staring up at me. "You have to skate!"

I shrugged. "I'm a nine."

He hoisted two pairs of skates to the counter as Katie watched, her eyes dancing. "Mine are pink!"

"They sure are," he told her. "Best ones we've got."

She clapped her hands and I dug out my wallet, but Arnold waved me off. "Part of the rink rental." I was surprised, but figured Sly probably didn't want to practice around a bunch of kids while he got ready for next season. It was probably normal hockey player behavior.

"Thank you." We headed to a bench on one side of the plexiglass, and I began helping Katie get her skates on.

"Where is Sillllvester?" she asked. "Ooh, these are heavy."

"They are," I told her. "And I don't—"

I heard him and felt him before I even saw him. The rhythmic shirring sound of skates on ice accompanied a movement of atmosphere that replaced the total stillness of the quiet rink, and I turned to see Sly on the ice, skating an easy circle around the ice and then gradually putting on speed until he was all but flying towards us. He stopped so suddenly I wouldn't have thought he could stay upright, shearing ice shards that flew toward the opening in the little wall around the rink. "You made it!" He sounded positively gleeful, and some of the wariness I'd been feeling slipped away.

"Silllvesster! My skates are pink!"

"That's the fastest color," he said seriously. "You sure you can handle pink? We could have Arnold get you some plain old black ones like mine." He lifted one of his feet to show her.

She shook her head. "Once I learn, I'll be faster than you."

He laughed. "We'll see." Then his warm eyes left my daughter, and Sly Remington's full attention was on me, sending my skin heating and want pooling inside me. His expression tightened, moving from the easy laughter he'd shared with Katie to something else, something darker that made me want to step closer but also warned me away.

"Hi Clara."

"Hi Sly."

"You don't have your skates on." His voice made me want to crawl toward him on my hands and knees and do whatever he asked of me.

I straightened, standing up to face him and cleared my throat. "I figured I'd let you and Katie get your lesson in first."

He nodded. "Sure. Your lesson can come later." There was a deeper meaning in his words, and a light shudder ran through me. Could it be that the desire we feel in youth never really leaves us? Maybe it's just dormant, gathering strength in the hidden corners of our hearts, waiting to spring to life later with an even fiercer, deeper pulse.

"You ready?" he asked my daughter, reaching for her hand.

She got to her feet carefully, her ankles wobbling as she stood on skates for the first time. "Oh!" she said, sounding surprised.

"Takes a little getting used to. But you have super strong legs, I bet, so you can do it." He nodded at her, encouragingly.

Katie's legs straightened a tiny bit, responding to Sly's suggestion. She picked up one skate and then the other, moving slowly toward his outstretched hand. "Okay," she said, sounding less confident than she had before.

"Let's do this," Sly said, his voice full of encouragement. "You'll be flying over the ice in no time."

"You sure?" she asked. Hearing Katie hesitate pulled at my heart. "I think it's harder than it looks."

"The best things are," Sly agreed, stepping through the little door and onto the ice and turning to take both of Katie's hands. "Just step on out here and we'll figure it out."

She did, so tentatively my heart squeezed with the fierce desire to go gather her into my arms and protect her. But this wasn't a real threat, and I knew Sly would take care of her. It was strange, realizing that. I trusted him with my daughter in a way I had never really trusted Zach, her own father.

I watched as he moved slowly backwards and she took her first skating steps. And then, as she got the feel of it, her steps became glides, until eventually, they were moving in a somewhat shaky circle around the ice and I felt myself relax.

Sly wore loose-fitting workout pants that hugged his butt and thighs, moving with his muscles as he flexed and shifted, and a short-sleeved T-shirt that was snug across his chest. Combined with the hockey skates, the carelessly waved dark hair, and the smile he was aiming at the little girl before him, he was the hottest guy I'd ever seen, and I found myself wishing for the same attention he was giving Katie.

He was kind and gentle as he talked to her and helped her find the right stance. His voice was low and encouraging, and though I couldn't hear all his words from where I sat, I heard the rumbling scratch of them, and it set parts of me aflame.

Here was a man who I'd never really thought I might have, treating my daughter so much better than her own father ever had. Taking time with her, being kind and patient. This was the kind of man I wanted.

Not the kind of man, my heart corrected. The man.

This was the man I wanted.

And that was a problem. Sly Remington was not a father figure. He wasn't a doting boyfriend or a potential husband. He didn't live here, and the life he had didn't fit the world we actually lived in.

Even as I watched him with Katie, I thought of the photos I'd seen of him with women—puck bunnies, I think they called them. Young, beautiful, shiny in a very specific kind of way that I thought took a lot of hours in front of a mirror and very small clothes. If those women were the kind he liked . . . why was he flirting with me?

Or was it all part of a game to him?

Sly shot me a smile then, catching my eyes as he skated backwards around the ice, holding Katie's hands. And in that instant, the fears and concerns I had backed away into the dark closet where I kept them. And the warm wanting of him returned.

They spent the better part of an hour together, with me sitting on the bench and watching, trying pointlessly not to love them both in desperate ways that made me feel so very vulnerable, and then Sly brought Katie back to me and I folded her into a hug. "You did so good, Bear."

"I did," she agreed. "Sly said next time I can learn how to spin."

By the time they'd left the ice, she was skating confidently on her own, but I doubted stunts were the natural progression from here. I nodded and smiled anyway.

"Your turn," Sly said, reaching out a hand.

I glanced at Katie, not sure I should leave her on her own.

"Anyone interested in checking out the Zamboni?" The man from the skate rental counter asked, appearing from down the side of the rink.

"What is a Zamboni?" Katie asked, wrinkling her nose. "Do you eat it?"

"Why don't I help you get your normal shoes on, and I'll show you. If it's okay with your mom." The man stretched out a hand. "I own the rink. I've known Sly here since he was about ten. He told me you're Clara. Ted Connor's daughter?"

I shook his hand and smiled. "You knew my dad."

"Good man."

"He was." I pushed down the sadness threatening to rise inside me.

"Can I show your daughter the Zamboni? We'll be right there." He pointed to the far side of the rink, where I assumed the Zamboni was kept.

"Sure. That's really nice of you."

"What is a Zamboni?" Katie asked again, struggling to untie her skates.

Sly dropped down to help her as I put my own skates on, and explained in a soft voice. "The coolest car you've ever seen. It's huge and it drives across the ice and makes it all shiny and smooth again."

She turned to look up at Arnold. "Will I get to drive?"

Arnold laughed. "We'll see, okay?"

She nodded. "I don't have a license."

He chuckled and they headed around the side of the rink. I turned back to Sly. "That's okay, you think?"

"I've known him forever. He used to drive me home after practice sometimes. He's got about ten kids of his own, I think. Loves 'em."

I nodded, and looked up into those deep caramel eyes. "Okay. Let's see if I remember how to skate."

I did. And for a little while, I moved carefully around the ice, staying close to the wall. I was a little wobbly, but my confidence came back slowly.

"You're doing great," Sly told me, sliding by like a dancer and then spinning around to face me as he skated backwards.

"Now you're just showing off," I teased.

"If I wanted to show off, I'd do this," he said, and a second later, he was racing away from me toward the center of the ice, where he performed some kind of jump I was pretty sure I'd only seen before in the winter Olympic figure skating competition.

I gasped and laughed with surprise, applauding him as he returned to me. His cheeks were flushed and his eyes sparkled. "I thought you played hockey. Maybe you have a better future as an ice dancer!"

"I took a few years of figure skating lessons," he said, grinning. He took my hands then, pulling me with him as he skated backwards again, and moved us toward the center of the rink. I did my best to focus on the movement of my feet instead of the hard callouses of Sly's palms against my own, the warmth of his skin, the nearness of his body.

I could hear the high pitch of Katie's laughter somewhere off to one side, but it was faint enough that I was in danger of becoming completely entranced by the man before me. By the warm, gentle way he held my hands. By the way his eyes drew me in as he asked, "Do you trust me, Clara?"

Nodding, I listened as he told me how to position my skates, and then he put his arms around my waist, pulling me against him. The warm, hard planes of his body matched to my curves, and I had the sensation of completion, of something aligning on a cosmic level. And then he began to spin us, and my arms gripped him tightly as a gleeful shriek left me.

"Oh my god!" I laughed, the world sliding by at increasing speeds until I slammed my eyes shut and buried my face against the warm reassurance of Sly's chest.

In that moment, I was sixteen again, worry and stress filtering away until all I knew was the joy of being held and spun, the pure ecstasy of possibility. Sly was holding me. I was the sole focus of his attention, and it was the best feeling I'd ever known.

We slowed, spinning gradually to a stop, and I stayed where I was, pressed tightly to his body, my arms around the firm solidity of his back. The exhilaration slowly faded, until I pulled my face from his chest and looked up into his face.

Sly wore a soft smile, his eyes deep and dark and full of something that looked a lot like desire. Without intending to, I licked my lips, my eyes dropping to focus on his full mouth.

He leaned in closer, our faces just centimeters away from one another, and then his lips met mine. Softly, carefully. He brushed my mouth like a whisper, tentative and sweet.

My arms tightened around him and I pressed myself closer, wishing for something I couldn't even name.

A soft low groan escaped him, and he deepened the kiss, sending heat pooling in my belly and lower. I wanted to climb inside his clothes, to ask him to take me here on the ice, to—

"Mommy! I'm driving!"

I wrenched myself from Sly's embrace, my breath coming too fast as I looked around to find Katie.

She and Arnold were perched atop the Zamboni at the end of the rink, and she waved triumphantly as the big machine moved slowly around the edge of the ice.

"Is that safe?" I asked Sly, trying to push away the intensity of the moment we'd just shared. I couldn't think about it now. I'd save it for later. When I was alone.

"With Arnold it is." I could feel his eyes on me as I watched my daughter happily moving around the ice on the Zamboni. "Let's get our skates off, yeah?"

"Okay," I said, and trailed him off the ice to put my street shoes back on. In some ways I still felt like I was spinning. Sly Remington had kissed me—held me. It was the realization of every teenaged dream I'd ever had about him, since my dreams were pretty chaste at that age. And I didn't know what happened next now any more than I would have then.

We returned our skates, thanked Arnold, and followed Sly out of the rink to stand in the damp heat of the parking lot. It had been easy to forget how hot it was outside when we were in the ice rink. It had been easy to forget a lot of things.

I looked up at him, squinting slightly in the late afternoon sunlight. I wasn't sure what to say, how to behave. There was no question that he had kissed me in there.

So why did it feel a bit like I made the whole thing up?

He smiled down at me, calm and casual as ever, that easygoing demeanor covering for any second thoughts or nerves he might have. All of which made it even easier to feel like maybe I'd imagined the tense moment between us at center ice. The kiss.

"Want to get some dinner before we head back?" Sly asked us.

"Hot dogs!" Katie had moved straight past the required yes or no and directly into negotiating for her favorite food.

Sly nodded like he was considering this, and looked to me. "Do you have time?"

"Yeah." Relief seeped through me that he'd been willing to take the lead, along with happiness that we'd be spending more time together.

"There's a place over here that probably has hot dogs. They have other things too, though."

Katie stomped her foot as if the very idea that a restaurant might dare to carry anything besides hot dogs was an affront to any self-respecting hot dog lover.

"That sounds good," I said. "Should we just follow you?"

Sly's lips lifted on one side and his nose wrinkled a bit. "I mean. You can, if you just like the view from behind, I guess. But I'm okay with you walking next to me too."

For one second, I was confused, but then I realized we were going to walk. "Funny."

Sly shrugged, and said, "let's go."

We did follow him, but only because the afternoon's excitement was hitting Katie, and she was having trouble getting her land legs back after wearing the skates.

"My legs feel funny."

"Your muscles are tired. You worked hard."

Luckily, we didn't walk far. The restaurant, Benny's Burgers, was practically next to the rink, and soon we were ensconced in a corner booth, and Katie had a set of crayons and an activity sheet in front of her.

I was about to ask Sly why he hadn't mentioned his plan to stay all summer when his phone rang, and he glanced at it, then frowned and answered, his eyes meeting mine in a silent apology.

"Hey," he said.

I stared down at the menu, trying not to eavesdrop.

"You're kidding." He sounded disappointed about something and I risked a look up at him. "Oh. You mean the calculations? Oh. Because I didn't do the projections right."

"You did. I know." He paused, rubbing his forehead for a brief second and taking a deep breath.

"Yeah, I just feel responsible. That was my part."

Now I heard defeat in his voice, and watched as his eyes slid shut and he dropped his head into his other hand as he held the phone to his ear.

Calculations and projections? This wasn't about hockey, I didn't think. It had to be the MBA.

He ended the call and put his phone away, took a breath and then said, "I'm thinking it's a milkshake day."

"Hey," I said. "What was that? Everything okay?"

Katie was absorbed in coloring, and it gave us a bit of privacy. I hoped he'd open up about whatever was clearly bothering him.

He sighed. "Not really. We just turned in a group project in my Data Visualization course, and the group didn't do very well. Because I screwed it up."

"Oh no." I understood what that felt like, the pressure of letting the team down.

"They probably expected it."

"Why would they expect to do poorly?"

"Because they got me. I suck at school, Clara. That's not a secret."

"It's also not a fact." I replayed his side of the conversation in my head. "They checked your work though, right?"

"Yeah."

"So this was a group error. It's not on you."

He blew out a frustrated breath, and dropped my gaze to stare down at his hand on the table for a moment.

"Hey," I said softly, hoping to draw his eyes back to mine. "Do you get another shot at it?"

"Yeah. We have a few days to redo the parts that were wrong. My parts."

"Can I help?"

He didn't answer me, and was clearly happy to see the waitress appear at the end of the table to take our orders. Had I overstepped? Or was this thing between us just a fleeting dalliance, was it just the one kiss but not meant to be part of the rest of our lives? The important parts? It was way too early to think about anything like that, but I knew Sly needed help. And he didn't want it from me.

We didn't talk about his classes again. Instead, Sly busied

himself helping Katie draw on her menu, playing tic tac toe and studiously dodging any conversation that might veer back to his studies. But I could see the hurt in the way he held himself, just slightly less sure than the man who'd kissed me on the ice.

I didn't want to see him looking defeated, but it was clear he wasn't looking for help. At least not from me.

CHAPTER 11
SLY

BACK IN A SLY-SHAPED BOX

J ust when I thought maybe I had a shot with Clara, just as I'd shown her some of who I really was, had maybe even impressed her a little, I'd been slammed right back into the Sly-shaped box I'd lived in my whole life. The one that kept me in my place, that made me remember I was just a dumb jock.

I was thrilled to be a successful player. It wasn't that I took the Wombats or my natural skills for granted. I didn't. I was thankful for every day I got on the ice.

But that wouldn't last, and I knew it.

And then where would I be?

A has-been. A guy who used to play.

I had plenty of money. My life would be good. But it would be empty. If I didn't have hockey, what did I have? The MBA would let me stay close to what I loved. Hopefully. But now?

Maybe Arnold would let me operate the Zamboni at his rink when I came home in shame and found a house near my folks. But I didn't relish the thought of a future spent driving a Zamboni around, living in the shadow of my past.

INTERLUDE

JULIUS RAMON (AKA ZAMBONI DRIVER)

Forgive the interruption, but as I represent the Zamboni-driving contingent in this particular story, I felt it was important to add here that some people really enjoy the thrill and responsibility of driving a Zamboni.

And while hockey cannot be one of those careers that sees you gently into your golden years, thanks to the sheer physicality of it, maintaining proximity to a thing you love is never the wrong choice.

But in this case, Zamboni husbandry is probably not the right thing for Sylvester Remington. I'd known the man a while now, and knew he had a particular tendency to discount himself any time his intelligence was the topic under consideration.

Why in the world people believe that men and women are either good at sports or intelligent is something I will never fully understand. But it's clear that Sly has bought that load of crap and has been living under its weight his whole life.

Maybe Clara can show him the way out.

CHAPTER 12
SLY

NOT CRYING IN MY CHILI

Clara and I said goodbye in the parking lot and pulled into our parallel driveways like synchronized swimmers, in tandem. The goodbye had been a little awkward after the kiss and then the phone call. I knew I hadn't reacted right to her offer of help, but that would just be too much like reliving the past, wouldn't it? Clara and me at the table, me struggling and her looking on, realizing moment by moment how thick I actually was. I didn't want her to see me that way.

When they'd gone inside, I should have gone in and gotten right to work, but I needed a few minutes to get my head back together, so I headed up the stairs next to the garage and let myself into the sweltering space above it.

It was still dusty and dirty up there, but it was the only place I could really escape to where no one would want to know why I wasn't cracking jokes or being my usual self. I knew why, even though I didn't really like to admit it.

I wasn't going to get an MBA, and I wasn't sure why I'd convinced myself I could. Maybe this single project wouldn't end things for me, but there'd be more like it. More teammates to let down, more professors who probably knew all along that I couldn't cut it.

I sank down into the old flower-patterned armchair next to the window and turned on the ancient air conditioner, which sputtered and groaned before settling into a steady hum.

This was why I didn't mention the program to anyone. That way, if I failed, I was the only one who'd know. I wasn't letting anyone close to me down, or confirming their expectations that I'd never hack it anyway. And thank god no one in the program knew who I really was, save maybe the administrators who admitted me in the first place, if they happened to watch hockey.

I was managing a good deep dwell on my own inadequacies when the phone in my pocket vibrated with a text. The darkness in my mind dissipated a tiny bit when I saw who it was.

Clara: Thanks for a fun day. Katie's exhausted!

Me: You're welcome. Thanks for coming.

I wanted to say something else, maybe ask her out on a proper date, but I realized she probably wouldn't want to do that. Especially not now that she'd had every suspicion she'd had about me since high school confirmed by a single phone call over dinner. Why had I told her about the program? Why had I told her anything?

Clara: I wondered if you wanted any help with
the assignment you have to redo?

Shit.

I was immediately transported back to high school, to the

feeling of complete and utter inadequacy while sitting across from the girl I wanted, the one I knew would never consider dating a dumb jock like me.

Clara was a goddamn scientist. She was fucking brilliant. And now she saw me as some kind of pathetic charity case all over again. It didn't make it better that my mom had been pulling strings to get us together from the start.

> Me: I doubt my mom would pay you for that, so I'm probably good.

> Clara: !! What is that supposed to mean?

I squeezed my eyes shut, at war with myself, and finally typed out.

> Me: Thanks for offering, but I'm fine. See you later.

The three dots danced on my screen for a minute, and I found myself almost desperate to receive her next words. But they didn't come.

And after five full minutes, the dots were gone and I shoved my phone back into my pocket, only to jump as it rang.

Assuming it would be her, I answered. "Hey."

"Hey Slick." Shit. Not Clara. Rock Stevens. He always seemed to catch me at my low points, which was why I considered him to be our second string team psych.

"What's good, Rock?"

"Life, man. Gotta love summertime." Rock sounded like he was living the dream. He was probably calling me from a lounger in his backyard pool, holding a beer in his other hand while Drea floated nearby in a bikini.

"Glad to hear it."

"Why do you sound like you've been crying in your chili?"

I cleared my throat and then cursed myself for practically confirming his suspicion. "I'm not."

"Uh huh. Okay."

"What's going on, Rock? I need to get going in a second here."

"As your captain, I'm just checking in. Officially making sure you'll be ready for the exhibition game next month and in top form."

"Got back on the ice today." Not that one skate with a five-year old and a kiss on center ice would quite count as being in top form.

"Good. That's good." He was quiet a moment. "You need to talk about something, man?"

"We are talking, asshole."

"Fine, be like that."

"You sound like you're five now."

"Five times better looking than you are? Five times faster? Five times smarter than you?"

That one hurt. "I gotta go."

"Hey, first—Mizzoni's having another barbecue next weekend if you're up for it."

"He's gonna let us back after Deck and Cade got crumbs all over his new couch?"

"He moved the PlayStation outside to the covered patio. He said we're not allowed in the house."

I burst out laughing, and it felt good to be distracted for a moment from my funk. "Of course he did."

"Saturday night, okay?"

"Yeah. Rock?" I hesitated, but it was worth a shot. "Cool if I bring someone?"

"Not if it's one of your usual someones. No one wants that drama. You're the reason we had to make a rule."

"It's not. She might not even come. It's just an old friend from home."

"The old friend you mentioned when we spoke the other night? Your high school wet dream?"

Leave it to Rock to make it sound dirty. "Um. Yeah, her."

"Sure."

"Thanks. See you there."

I hung up and stared at the space around me. I didn't know if Clara would even want to come with me. That'd be something awfully close to a date, and hanging out with the team could be a lot for just about anyone. Especially someone who didn't suffer from delusions about hockey players in general or spend their lives trying to get on the inside of a team like the Wombats. Plus, Clara had just gotten a close-up view to the real Sly Remington, close enough to know nothing had changed despite the pro status and the money.

She probably wouldn't want to come. Maybe I wouldn't even ask her.

CHAPTER 13
CLARA

MAMA'S ON THE MOVE

The next day I was at work early, Katie at pre-care at school, and my brain still circling around Sly's text response to my offer to help him with school.

"What is happening here?" My partner Betty asked me, gesturing to my entire body as we parked the truck and got ready to head out for the day.

"What here?"

"Here. With you." She pointed to her head, where her blue-streaked dark hair was pulled into a tight ponytail she was dropping a hat on top of.

"Sorry. Nothing." I shook my head. I needed to be clear for work. We'd placed an orphan with a mama in late winter, and though all had been going well, one of the cameras near the den had been knocked out by a storm. We needed to check on the mama and get the camera turned back in the right direction. I needed my brain on track for all that.

"You're sure?" She frowned at me as she double-checked her pack.

"Yeah, I'm sorry. Just had a weird weekend is all."

"What weird?" she said, strapping on the pack and then

coming to face me as I finished my own prep. My pack was going to be a little heavier with the ladder we needed to carry.

"Nothing really, just . . ."

"The guy. The hockey player you told me about?" I'd told her last week about Sly next door, our history. His ongoing shirtless hotness.

"Yeah. We hung out a little bit this weekend. He's teaching Katie to skate."

"That's cute," Betty said, though her words didn't sound too sincere. Betty was not a fan of children. She was nice enough to Katie, but didn't plan on having any of her own, and was not charmed by stories of the antics of kids.

"Yeah, it was. And then Katie was hanging out with the owner of the rink a little bit, and Sly took me out on the ice." I endowed the words with a little more drama than was strictly necessary.

Now I had her attention. As we locked the truck and started the hike into the forest, I could feel Betty's interest spike. "And?"

"And we kissed."

Betty squealed. "So you made out with a star hockey player."

Something about her words made it feel a little less incredible than it had been, sleazy somehow. "I mean, yeah. It was quick, but it was . . .wow."

"Just the one kiss? Why'd you stop?"

"Kid," I said and Betty rolled her eyes. "I've wanted to kiss Sly Remington since I was in ninth grade."

"Oooh, I love it. Will there be more kissing?"

I thought about that. I wanted there to be. But Sly had shut down completely when he'd gotten the news about school. It reminded me so much of when we were younger, the way he'd beat himself up over tests in high school. "I don't know," I said.

"Yeah you do," she told me, looking disappointed in me. "Clearly he's into you. If you want more, make it happen."

"It's complicated."

"Don't say because of Katie." It was, though. Because of Katie, and because of Zach. I'd already spent years with a guy who didn't want me to be me. And Sly had already demonstrated his disapproval of my job, which had done very little to quell my interest in him. Because obviously, I only liked guys who didn't want me as I was.

I ducked under a branch, and we skirted around a fall of boulders. The bear's den was about four miles in, but if the bears were out foraging, we could bump into them at any point if we weren't paying attention. Betty held the tracker, pinpointing the bear on the GPS screen. Looked like Mama was staying close to the den, so we could stay on a relatively straight course.

"No, not because of Katie. Because of all kinds of other stuff. And now he's staying all summer."

"All the more reason to let things progress. See what's there."

"I guess, but there's part of me that thinks he might have just kissed me because it was easy and I was there. Because it was probably so obvious that I wanted him to."

She made a disapproving sound and shook her head. "Honey, you are so fucking hot and you don't even know it. He kissed you because you're a smoke show, not because he had nothing better to do. And if you had a crush on him in high school? I'd bet money it went both ways."

"I don't think so." Flashes of the homecoming queen scattered through my mind. "I'm not his type."

Betty sighed, leaving me to think about the last chat I'd had with Sly. I shouldn't have offered to help him with school. It probably made him think I didn't believe in him, in his intelligence.

He'd said something when we were young about having a sophomore tutoring him, and how it just proved he was a moron . . . why would he be any happier to have me offer now? Of course, at the time, I'd thought it was a dig on me somehow, that he was pointing out what a nerd I was or something.

Weird how when you're young, you can't see past the way words and ideas sting and bruise you, not even noticing if they're slicing someone else to bits.

Maybe Sly felt insecure about his intelligence around me

because of our past? It seemed like a stretch, but it did explain his shutdown via text.

"Mama's on the move," Betty said, and I moved to where she held the tracker, watching the flashing red dot move slowly away from us.

"Good." We were still a couple miles out from the den, but hopefully the bears would be away the whole time, making our jobs pretty easy.

"How can I let him know I want more?" I asked her, my mind still flipping over Sly's last texts the previous night.

"Do you want to? I mean . . . the guy's going back to hockey soon, right? It's not like he'll be sticking around."

"He's staying all summer," I reminded her.

"Are you okay with being a summer fling?"

"Honestly?" I thought about it. "I want to say no, but that might be perfect. It isn't like I have time for anything else anyway."

"Then you should ask him out. Stash the kid somewhere and give him some time to make a proper move."

I thought about that. It still felt wrong—putting myself out there for Sly. The insecure teenager who could only talk about equations with the hot hockey player still lived within me, but I didn't think Sly would appreciate me speaking in theorems at this point.

"Shoot, Mom's coming back this way," Betty said, and I peered at the dot on the GPS moving our way.

"Crap." We switched direction, heading up a steep slope to skirt around to the den from the other side. Running into the bear wouldn't be the end of the world, but it added a bit of excitement to the day we weren't necessarily hoping for. Especially because mamas could be protective when their cubs were around. True for human mamas too.

As we moved closer to the den, I thought about Sly. Did I want to invest myself more in a situation that was inevitably going to end? I'd been alone since Katie's dad took off, maybe not happily so, but we were fine. Still, the idea of spending more time with Sly was appealing. Not just because of my lifelong crush on the man, though that was part of it.

The adult version of Sly Remington was kind and sweet, sexy and fun. I'd be attracted to him even if I hadn't known him most of my life.

Doubt crept in. But was he honestly attracted to me? I definitely wasn't his usual type, judging by the photos I'd seen. Maybe I was just convenient while he was home for the summer.

The question was, would that be okay with me? To be a convenient summer diversion? It would be fun, no doubt about that. But could I keep my heart from getting broken in the process?

I sighed, peering through the shadowy canopy in front of us as the idea of being just a passing fancy pricked at me. I startled slightly as my phone buzzed in my pocket.

"Settle down," Betty said, smiling at me. "Bear's at least a half mile that way." She pointed downslope.

"Phone," I said, slipping it from my shorts pocket to see if it was about Katie. I was glad to have service. Sometimes I got back to the truck at the end of the day to find out Katie was sick and Violet had to go pick her up. One more reason why a shift in daily duties would be welcome.

The text was from Paul at headquarters. My heart leapt into my throat, but just as I was about to open it, another appeared. From Sly.

Sly: Got plans for Saturday?

My pulse quickened.

"It's him. He's asking about Saturday."

Betty gave me a quick nod. "Date. No kid."

Me: Not really, why?

Sly: There's a little team BBQ. Would love to take you. I'll understand if you don't want to go.

Me: Why wouldn't I want to go?'

Sly: No bears to wrestle, etc.

Me: Hmm . . . You're right. Might be a little boring.

Three dots danced and then disappeared, then danced again. Finally, Sly's reply came.

Sly: I'll wrestle with you if you want.

My heart slammed against my ribs. He was definitely flirting. That was suggestive, wasn't it?

"Betty!" I whispered. "Read this."

Betty read the text string, and a smile stretched her red lips wide as she began to nod. "Ooh, there's zero doubt he's into you. You see that, right?"

"Shit. What do I say?"

She rolled her eyes like I was the most exhausting and clueless friend she had.

"Just ask what time you need to be ready. And tell him where you're going to stash the kid and slip in that she'll be gone all night."

"I don't have an overnight babysitter!" There was no way I could ask Violet to sit all night so I could have sex with her son.

Betty sighed deeply and took her cap off, smoothing her hair before replacing it. "I might have told my sister I'd watch her six-year-old daughter overnight Saturday. Katie can come too. We'll have a slumber party."

I stared at her. Betty? As a babysitter? "You're serious?"

"If it means you get some action, I'll do this thing for you. But you will owe me."

Could I really leave Katie with Betty so I could hopefully spend the night with Sly? Giddy bubbles released inside me, making me dizzy for a second.

"Okay." I blew out a breath, trying to calm my nerves. "Thank you!"

"Don't let me down," she teased, a smile in her eyes.

Me: Sounds good. Katie's got a sleepover
Saturday so I'll be on my own. What time?

Sly: So that's a yes to wrestling?

Me: It's a yes to the BBQ. We'll go from there.

Sly: I'll pick you up at six.

I suppressed the gleeful shriek I wanted to let go, and shoved my phone back into my pocket instead. We had a job to do.

"There it is," Betty said, pointing up to where the camera was mounted on a tree trunk, about ten feet up. It was hanging at an odd angle.

I pulled off my pack, which had a telescoping ladder attached to it, and we set it up on the tree. Betty climbed up, readjusting the camera to focus back on the den, which was tucked beneath a rocky outcropping. I kept an eye on the GPS tracker, making sure we wouldn't have surprise company while Betty was working. It was never fun to have to use bear spray or tranquilizers in a situation like this.

The cubs weren't tagged, but this far into the summer, they were unlikely to be far from their mother, so there was no reason to risk climbing into the den to check on them as we'd done earlier in the spring.

"Got it," Betty said, and then she climbed down and we packed the ladder back up.

We checked the GPS to ensure mama bear wasn't in our path back to the truck, and headed off through the trees. As we reached the vehicle, and loaded back up, Betty came around, holding the tracker. The little dot that indicated mama bear was just inside the tree line now, maybe twenty-five feet from where we stood. We climbed into the truck and watched as the whole family wandered by, mama giving the truck a quick raised-head sniff and then hustling three cubs back into the brush. My heart soared and I felt the grin spread over my face. I couldn't help it. I loved this part of my job.

As we drove back, my focus was on the forest around us and the bears we took care of from a distance, but thoughts of being alone with Sly kept slipping in and tiny sparks of excitement flickered inside me.

We headed back to headquarters in the afternoon, and when I stepped inside the office, I checked the message I'd gotten just before Sly's text had popped up, distracting me. I hoped it would be news about the job.

I slid into my desk, listening to the message, which was from my boss.

His stern voice sounded slightly warped in the message. "Come see me when you get back from the field today."

That could be anything, really. I had messages like that most days. But with my application under final consideration for the supervisory position, I suspected I knew what it was about. If not what the outcome of my hopes might be.

"Clara, come in." Paul smiled as I knocked on the frame of his office door.

"Hey," I said, stepping inside.

"Wanna close that for a second?" he nodded toward the door, and I pulled it shut and then sat across his desk from him. "How'd it go in the field today?"

"Fine. We fixed the camera that got knocked out by the storm. The whole family wandered by it when we were heading back in. Looks like Mom and babies are doing well."

"That's good." He nodded and cleared his throat. "Well, enjoy this week in the field, Clara, because I'm afraid it'll be your last."

"Wha—?" Horror settled over me. He was firing me? "I'm sorry?"

"Yep. Next week you'll be riding a desk in your very own office right next door to me." He pointed a thumb to his right.

Cool relief replaced the sudden fear that had swept through me. "I got it?"

"You got it. The choice was clear. Congratulations."

Regular hours. An office job. No more cell phone cutting out, no more being away from Katie long hours. "That's wonderful, thank you!"

"You deserve it," he said. His voice was warm, and I took a second to absorb the emotions washing through me. I'd expected to be ecstatic, thrilled, even. But I wasn't. And though it was always a compliment to be selected, I felt a strange twist of disappointment.

"Okay, so . . . Monday?" I asked Paul.

"Monday."

"Thanks," I said again, rising.

"Just try to get things wrapped up in your notes, but since it isn't like you'll be leaving, it's not too critical."

"I will," I said. "Anything else?" I paused at the door.

"Enjoy your last week in the field. You'll tell Betty?"

I will. My partner would be bummed, I knew, but I had no doubt she'd have a new partner who would be great. The weird thing might be answering to me as a supervisor for fieldwork.

I looked for Betty outside, but she'd already gone for the night. That would give me time to figure out how to tell her. She knew I'd been interviewing, but had kept quiet about how she felt about it.

As I drove home, a text popped up.

Sly: Hi.

I used CarPlay to speak a reply.

Me: Hi.

Sly: Busy tonight?

Me: Not really, why?

Sly: Wondered if I could take you up on your offer of help with school.

Surprise made me straighten up slightly. Sly wanted help? I had definitely not seen that coming. I'd even been thinking of ways I might apologize for offering, on the chance it had made it seem like I didn't believe in him somehow.

Me: Of course.

Sly: Want to come here?

Me: Katie's been out all day, I'd like to be home.
Come to our house. I made enchiladas.

I'd made them Sunday and just needed to heat them up.

Sly: Sounds good. Thanks.

Me: I'll be home in ten minutes. See you in a half
hour?

Sly: Perfect.

I couldn't think of the last time I'd had a man over to the house, if I ever even had. Of course Zach had been to my parents' place a few times. He'd called it "small," though when we were dating he'd said it was "charming." His dislike of the house was part of the reason it had sat empty when my parents died, one after the other. The house was mine, and it was paid off, but it didn't meet Zach's standards. And when we separated, I'd stayed in the house we'd shared in Boomsmack, trying to see if things might work out. I was glad I hadn't sold the place as he'd suggested so many times.

It wasn't big, that was true. But it was similar to the house where Sly grew up and I didn't have any concerns about his impressions of my house. To me, it represented home and family. And in so many ways, my parents were still there. Around me.

When I pulled into the driveway, Katie came bounding down the steps next door, and I'd barely gotten the door open before she was talking a million words a minute.

"Sillllvesssster played dolls with me, Mommy, and then he let me sit on him while he did pushups and he let me punch him a whole bunch, and we had grilled cheese and watched a hockey game on TV!"

I looked up to see Violet waving from her doorstep.

"Thank you!" I called, taking Katie's hand and ushering her inside the house.

Sly had been hanging out with Katie all day?

"What was Violet doing while you were hanging out with Sly?" I knew Violet loved the time she spent with Katie and wondered if it had been fun for her to see her son with my daughter.

"She was baking cookies and stuff. She was there too."

I smiled. "Sounds like you had a great day."

She nodded.

"Would it be okay if Sylvester comes for dinner?"

She clapped her hands together. "Yes."

I put the enchiladas into the oven to heat and went to take a quick shower, feeling more excited than I should about helping Sly with his schoolwork.

If I was honest with myself, I was hoping for a lot more than dinner and homework.

SLY

LET'S TALK ABOUT CORN

I saw Clara's car pull in and did my best to give her a solid half hour to unwind from work. Who knew what kind of recovery a person needed after wrestling bears and rolling around in mud all day?

She pulled open the door before I even knocked, and hit me with a warm smile that almost knocked my feet out from under me. Katie slammed into me with a full-body hit to the legs, and that one practically did take my legs out from under me.

"Careful champ," I told her, reaching down to lift her up and set her against my hip. "You just may have a future wrestling bears like your mom."

"I don't—" Clara started to argue, but Katie was already talking. Loudly.

"I'm not gonna be a biologist. I'm gonna be a hockey player. Like you."

Clara gave her an indulgent smile and reached for her, but I shook my head. "I've got her. We need to talk about hockey anyway," I said.

"You sure? Sounds like you two spent the whole day together already."

We had. And it had actually been one of the best days in recent memory.

"You can never get enough tea parties with the queen," I told her.

"Oh no. I didn't even hear about that part." Clara laughed as she moved into the kitchen and I followed her, settling at the table with Katie on my lap.

"You didn't tell your mom about the queen?" I asked her.

Katie smiled up at me. "I don't tell my mom everything, Silll-lvester."

"How was work?" I asked. Clara was bustling around, pulling a tray of enchiladas from the oven and then tossing a salad on the island. "Hey, can I help?"

"You're keeping the trip hazard contained. That is help," she said. "And work was . . . it was good."

"Hesitation," I observed, my interest piqued. She tucked her hair behind her ear, a tiny smile on her lips. "Something's up."

"I got the promotion today." She said this more quietly, as if she didn't want to scare it away by stating it too loudly.

"Of course you did," I said. "Congratulations!"

She held a spatula in the air and gave me a funny look, tilting her head sideways. "What do you mean, of course I did?"

"You're fu—" I paused, looking at the little blond girl in my lap. "You're crazy smart. Always have been. I think you'll get anything you decide you want."

She pressed her lips into a half smile. "Well that's a nice thing to say."

"Just truth." I stood up, setting Katie down and looking around the kitchen. "Should we celebrate? Do you have champagne?" I wished I'd known earlier. I would have brought champagne. And flowers, maybe.

"I don't. It's okay."

I looked into the big eyes of the little girl at my side and winked at her and then put my finger to my lips, telling her not to blow my secret, as I pulled out my phone. I could fix this.

"Okay, time for dinner. It's a serve-yourself affair," Clara said, waving toward the plates on the counter. "Here, Katie." She filled a plate for Katie, who was looking more annoyed by the second.

"I can do it." Katie went to the side of the refrigerator and retrieved a step stool and then climbed up next to her mother and inspected the plate she'd prepared. "Too much salad."

"Eat what you can."

"I don't like this cheesy thing."

"That's an enchilada. There's chicken."

"I don't want it."

"Do you want to go straight to bed?"

Silence. I watched as Katie climbed down from her stool and reached for her plate, carrying it to the table. Clara placed a glass of milk, a fork and a napkin next to her, and I surmised that the standoff was over.

I marveled at how Clara took it all in stride, handling the challenge of getting a five-year old to eat as easily as she must wrestle her workday challenges, even if they weren't bears.

"You're good at everything," I whispered to Clara, thinking about how impressive she really was. "You're smart, funny, killing it at work, a kickass mom . . ."

"Um . . . thanks. Overstating."

I shook my head. "I don't think so. You've always been incredible."

She met my eyes then, wrinkling her nose at me. "What does that mean? In high school I was just the tutor girl next door. You barely knew I existed."

I held her gaze, hoping she'd see my sincerity there. "Oh, I definitely did, Clara."

A soft pink blush rose in her cheeks, and it took everything in me to reach for a plate instead of for her. I wanted to show her exactly how much I'd thought about her then, and how much I'd been thinking about her now. Especially since the kiss in the center of the ice.

"This looks incredible," I said. "Add amazing cook to the list."

"It's not very good, Silly Sylvester," Katie called to me from the table. "Very goopy."

"I love goopy enchiladas," I told Katie, smiling at Clara before I carried my plate to the table.

"These are yucky," Katie told me. I could tell she was hoping for a little conspiracy of dissatisfaction, and as much as I wanted to make Katie happy, the food looked amazing. I waited for Clara to join us, my stomach rumbling audibly.

Once Clara had sat down and lifted her fork, I took a bite, making a big show of enjoying it. It wasn't hard, because the food was amazing. "These are delicious," I said, meaning it and nodding at Katie.

"And Katie?" Clara said, her voice low with warning. "Do you remember what we talked about? When someone cooks for you?"

Katie dropped her mother's gaze and her shoulders slumped a bit. I wanted to reach out and scoop her up, but I knew these were the kinds of lessons that were important.

"This looks delicious, Mommy." Katie murmured the words, her shame at having been corrected almost palpable as Clara and I shared a knowing look.

I lifted my water toward the beautiful woman across from me. "To Clara. Congratulations on the job!"

Her brow furrowed for a split second before she smiled. "Thanks."

Katie was very absorbed in disassembling the items on her plate like some kind of culinary scientist, and I looked across the table. "You don't seem thrilled about the job."

Clara sighed. "No. I am."

"No. You're not." I took a bite, the flavors exploding on my tongue and distracting me momentarily. But it didn't take an expert to figure out something about the job bothered Clara. "What's up?"

She shook her head lightly. "Nothing. It's the right move. Work from home flexibility, office hours that'll keep me close to a phone and closer to Katie. Less uncertainty overall, and a better paycheck."

"Sounds perfect."

"It is."

"No wrestling with wildlife?"

She was quiet just long enough to tip me off that I'd hit the nail on the head. "Yeah. No more bears. I mean, I'll still be analyzing the data and tracking activity, building the reports and keeping tabs on all the bears."

But she wouldn't be in the field. I could see why she wasn't excited. She was doing the right thing. But it didn't seem like the right thing for her. "Don't take it," I suggested.

Surprise lifted her eyebrows as she looked up at me. "It's a promotion. Better money, more availability for Katie."

Katie had pushed her food into piles across her plate and was currently picking out a kernel of corn with her thumb and forefinger, leaning in close with a look of utter disgust painted across her little features. "Corn," she moaned.

"It sounds like you won't have as much fun at work."

"Life is not always about having fun. We can't all make a living playing games."

"Ouch." I dropped her gaze, the truth of that statement settling heavy in my gut. If I had any other skills, maybe it wouldn't have been such a direct hit. But she had a point. There wasn't much else I was capable of.

"Hey." Her voice softened, and I looked up, swallowing my hurt. "That's not what I meant. But I need to take this job. It just makes sense."

"Sure."

"You know what doesn't make sense?" Katie asked us both, oblivious to the parallel conversation going on around her. "Corn. It's good when it's popped and then like this . . . ugh."

Clara shot me a look that warned me not to engage, so I stifled my chuckle and kept eating.

We finished the meal without much more conversation, and I

did my best to shake off the grump that was threatening as we got closer to the reason I was at Clara's house in the first place. The quickly dwindling possibility that I'd pass this course and stay on track to get my MBA. That, and the increasing likelihood that I'd let down the entire group, jeopardizing everyone's chances of passing.

"I can clear the dishes," I said, taking plates to the sink.

"That would be really nice, if you don't mind," Clara answered. "I'll get Katie tucked in and then we can look at your project."

"No problem. Goodnight Kate the Great."

"I'm not going to bed," Katie declared, coming to stand next to me with her arms crossed as if I was on her side.

"You sure about that?" I bent down and picked her up, tossing her over my shoulder as she shrieked. "Which way to the bedroom?"

Katie was cackling hysterically and slapping my back while her little legs kicked, and Clara shot me a smile and pointed down the hall. I tried not to glance into Clara's room as I passed it. I had enough trouble with thinking about getting her into bed without actually seeing her bed.

I plopped Katie on her own little bed, which was covered with a comforter featuring Bob the Builder, something I would not have guessed, and then stood up. I crossed my arms just as she had. "See? You're in bed."

Clara followed me into the room, chuckling.

"I'm not even wearing pajamas!" Katie cried, slithering out of the bed and pulling open a drawer on her dresser.

"You get ready and then I'll come tell you goodnight," I suggested. "If that's okay with your mom."

"That's fine. Thanks for the assist."

I gave her a little salute and went back to finish the dishes.

It was strange to me suddenly that I'd never noticed how quiet and empty my regular life was. Clara, by contrast, had Katie to fill her days and nights with laughter and love . . . Mom had

Dad . . . Beckett had Zara . . . Shit, even Rock Stevens had settled down. I had a good life, a big apartment in the city, great teammates, sex pretty much whenever I wanted it. But something about being in this home, being with Katie and Clara—it felt more real. More important. Like this was what life was supposed to be about.

I dropped my hands to the counter and leaned forward to take a deep breath. I was good. Life was good.

Just then, Katie called to me. "Silly, come tuck me in!"

I went back and pulled Katie's comforter up around her chin, Clara looking on from beside me. "Goodnight, Katie-Bell."

"Goodnight Silly Sylvester." Katie wrapped her arms around my neck, pulling me close to inhale her sweet little-girl scent, and then I headed back out to the living room, feeling slightly off balance.

The doorbell rang as my phone vibrated with a text while Clara was still finishing tucking Katie in. "I'll grab it," I called to Clara, and then I headed to the door to meet the delivery person.

Fifteen minutes later, Clara came out to the living room, her thick blond hair pulled into a twist behind her head, and her face shining. Her feet were in slippers, and something about the way she looked in that moment pulled the same strings that had been getting tugged all night. I wanted to see her this way more. Relaxed. Comfortable. At home.

"Hey," I said, standing and handing her a glass of champagne. Her eyes widened, and then moved past me to land on the enormous bouquet of lilies. "I hope you like lilies."

"Sly," she said, her voice full of wonder. "Where did this all come from?"

I lifted a shoulder. "Delivery. You deserve to celebrate. Congratulations on the promotion, Clara. I'm proud of you."

Her eyes met mine and held for a long moment, and my heart caught in my throat. The deep blue eyes I'd begun to see in my dreams were shining and disbelieving.

We touched our glasses together and drank, and then she put

hers on the table, laughing. "This is . . . a lot," she said. "Thank you."

"You're welcome."

"If I drink this, I won't be much help to you with your project."

"Can't make it worse." Part of me wanted to forget the stupid project and see where a glass of champagne might lead us, but I knew it was important. And that was why we were here in the first place.

"Let's take a look." Clara gestured to the table.

I opened my laptop and spread the data and my analysis on the table, and we sat down to work. She spent some time reviewing and reading while I drank champagne, and then faced me. "I think I see the issue. It's not a big deal at all, but I also see why your teammates might have missed it in a quick review. It looks right. It's just this one little thing here."

Just as she had in high school, Clara explained the complexities of the work in a way I understood easily. She used examples and also made a point to praise what I'd done. I was transported back to being seventeen again, and I sat in quiet awe of the woman across from me.

After a few minutes, she stopped speaking, and I realized I hadn't heard much of the last few words because my mind had gone other places.

"Sly?"

"Yeah?"

"I asked you a question. About this?" She pointed to the graph that lay between us.

"Yes."

"That's not the right answer." Her eyes had snagged on mine again, and while a little smile flickered across her face, I was certain I saw something else in her expression. Something I was pretty sure was matched in my own.

I leaned in a tiny bit. "Tell me if this is the right answer." I moved even closer, and she didn't move away, didn't drop my gaze. She sucked in a sharp breath as my lips met hers, and I slid my hand along the side of her face, cupping her jaw.

It was everything I'd imagined from the brief kiss on the ice, but now, in the quiet of her living room, there was little chance of a Zamboni-fueled interruption.

I deepened the kiss, pulling her to me, my other hand finding her hip. Clara didn't hesitate, rising and then stepping closer without breaking contact. A second later, she was wrapping herself around me as I sat, one of her legs falling to either side of my hips, as I fought to control myself. It would do no good to throw her on the table and take her like a cave man. This kiss already far exceeded my high school dreams, and was more leisurely and savoring than our kiss on the ice, and I wasn't going to rush anything.

I pulled her close to me, giddy at the way her arms wrapped around my neck as her center pressed into me, adding pressure to the suddenly iron-hard length of my erection. Her tongue darted out, teasing me, and I groaned, slanting my lips to increase the contact.

Time stopped.

The room spun around us.

Tongues and breath mingled as Clara rubbed herself against me, hard, forcing my breath to come faster as I fought for control.

Kissing Clara Connor was everything I'd ever imagined and so much more. I didn't know if it was that Clara was an adult woman and not an inexperienced teenager, or if kissing her would have been every bit as fantastic years ago when I'd first had the idea. All I knew was that this single kiss far surpassed every kiss I'd had previously, maybe because I'd never really cared about anyone I'd dated in the past.

Without a spoken word, I stood, pulling Clara with me. We were communicating, but it wasn't in syllables. It was in desperate pulls on each other's clothing, with pained groans, and hammering hearts. I walked Clara backwards to the couch, where

I laid her down and then carefully aligned myself with her body, desperate to be close but also not eager to crush her.

Her arms wrapped me, her hands tracking up and down my back, squeezing my ass, pulling me closer and closer to her until thrusting was the only thing I could do to relieve some of the building tension. My mouth and hips fell into a kind of rhythm, and the breathy moans Clara was releasing spurred me on.

This was like a championship dry hump, and I had a fleeting thought that my high-school self would have been pretty excited about the whole thing.

But my adult self was desperate to get Clara's clothes off, to sink myself into her and finally, finally attempt to sate my desire for this incredible woman.

This, however, was not the time or place for that. There was an adorable little girl just feet away.

I heaved my body back to the opposite end of the couch, adjusting my over-eager cock and doing my best to catch my breath.

"Wha—? Um . . ." Clara's eyes were glassy, and her chest rose and fell rapidly as she looked at me.

I stroked her leg, letting my fingers slide up the smooth skin of her shin beneath the wide leg of the soft pants she wore. "I needed to get hold of myself before I fucked you silly right here on your couch."

"I think I was ready for that."

Parts of me thrilled to hear that news and did their level best to drive me right back to the brink of self-control, but I wasn't going to do it. "Not the right time," I managed to say, considering the possibility that I was the dumbest man alive for not taking the opportunity when I had it.

"Oh." Was I imagining the disappointment in her voice? "Yeah, I mean . . . Katie's a great sleeper, but it takes her a little while to get there."

Right. And Katie didn't need a rated-X education at five years old. I certainly didn't want to be responsible for giving it to her.

And the things I wanted to do to her mother if given the chance . . . well, privacy would be required.

I rubbed my hands through my hair, and then laughed, looking at Clara. "I promise I didn't come over here tonight planning to attack you on the couch."

She sat up and adjusted her tank top, giving me a look so sexy and shy I wanted to tackle her all over again. "I didn't mind," she said, sending my heart leaping around inside me. "Can I tell you something?"

Her uncertainty . . . the shy way she asked me this, dropping my eyes and then catching them again from beneath her thick lashes . . . I didn't think I could actually be more turned on, but she proved me wrong. "Yeah." It was a growl.

"I've had a crush on you since high school. That"—she nodded toward the couch we'd come close to christening—"pretty much fulfilled every teenaged fantasy I ever had."

Shock trickled through me, making my fingers tingle with pleasure. "You're kidding."

She shook her head, a little smile on her lips. I scooted close and cupped her jaw again, loving the way she pressed into my hand, her eyes dropping shut like just the feel of me was too much for her.

"Well, we wasted a lot of time then. Because that high school crush?" Her eyes popped open, met mine. "Was completely mutual." The eyes widened in surprise.

"No it wasn't."

"It was."

"You never said anything. I was dying for you to ask me out."

"I couldn't." I could have, but it would have meant risking rejection. "You were way out of my league." Honestly, she still was.

She straightened. "You were a star athlete. Everyone wanted to go out with you. Sly, literally no one was out of your league."

I chuckled. "As nice as it is to hear that . . . you were. And you probably still are. I'm just tired of fighting it."

She shook her head. "Don't fight it."

I stared at her, still in shock that I was sitting here, in Clara Connor's living room, my thumb tracing light lines along her perfect cheek as her deep blue eyes stared into mine with desire. "You've always been way too good for me."

She sat up, her expression clearing as her head left my hand. "You're insane. You spent your day playing dolls and having tea parties with a five-year old. You ordered champagne and flowers out of nowhere to celebrate a promotion you just found out about. You gave up your summer to help your dad rebuild an old fence . . ."

"Let's be clear. I gave up a summer to see if there was any chance with the girl next door."

Clara's mouth dropped open slightly. "Wait, seriously?"

I shrugged. "And to hang out with my family. Dad's not doing great, you know?"

She nodded, said quietly, "I know."

"But mostly to roll the dice on this. I didn't think there was much of a chance."

"You're crazy."

I nodded. "Yeah. Maybe."

Clara laughed and moved toward me, pressing herself against my chest. My arms wrapped around her, and it felt like she was right where she belonged, like these arms were made for this.

"Do you think we should finish this project?" she asked.

"Oh, I don't know. I think it might take all week."

Clara laughed and I held her like that for a long time, trying to memorize the way it felt to hold her, the soft vanilla scent of her, the way her body moved with each breath.

I'd kissed her only a couple of times, and I already knew I was in way too deep to walk away unscathed.

CHAPTER 15
CLARA

PLAYING FAVORITES

Kissing Sly Remington was eighteen thousand times better than it had been in the last decade of imagining it. Back in my high school days, I'd pictured him demanding and directive, forceful and strong. And while there had been moments where he was all of those things (like when he pushed me into the couch and laid me down there . . . sigh), he'd been attentive and careful by equal measure. I now had zero doubt that sex with Sly would be unlike any experience I'd had before. Not that I'd had many.

But Saturday night seemed like the night when I'd finally find out.

The thought made me giddy and nervous, and I spent my last week out in the field distracted by quick texts back and forth with him.

I also spent it happy, despite my reluctance to leave Betty and my bears while I sat in an office.

"I'm going to miss you," Betty said when I'd told her. "And I'm not going to call you boss."

"Fair," I agreed.

"But the truth is, you'll be great. And I'd rather report to you than Paul any day. Less anecdotes about smoking meat, at least."

"Guaranteed. I don't even know how to smoke meat."

"I think you just roll it in some paper and light it . . . but don't inhale too deeply."

"Funny." I grinned at Betty as we drove back to the office that Friday.

"So we'll see you tomorrow? Like four o'clock?"

Betty gave me a thumbs up. "I've already got the Barbie mansion set up and every Disney princess movie queued."

"Sounds perfect," I said. I'd enrolled Katie in every science and construction camp I could find for kids her age, but despite her devotion to dump trucks and forklifts, she also loved glitter and Barbie. I'd actually seen her wear a tool belt while hosting teddy bear tea parties. She was a perfect blend of fascinating interests.

We'd finished up our fieldwork early, and I was heading home instead of putting in a few more hours. I could catch up when I reported for my new job Monday. Until then, I was too distracted for work.

And when I got home, I was rewarded.

Sly was standing in between our driveways at the start of the fence that normally separated our backyards. Over the course of the week, the fence had slowly disappeared as he and Sam had pulled it down. Now he held some kind of equipment, and every muscle in his (shirtless!) back was flexing as he worked it into the ground.

I practically swallowed my tongue when I first spotted him, but I'd gotten it together before I approached, waiting for him to take a break before interrupting.

"Hey," I called.

Sly looked up and then turned to face me in all his shirtless glory. He wore a pair of athletic shorts slung low and a Wilcox Wombats cap to shade his face, but it didn't hide the wide smile he gave me when he spotted me.

"Hello supervisor," he said. He'd been calling me that all week in quick texts, since he learned of my promotion.

"This looks pretty serious." I pointed at the heavy machine he'd been using.

"We rented an augur to dig the holes for the new posts."

I looked around, but didn't see Sam. As if reading my mind, Sly said, "Dad didn't feel great, so I sent him inside to rest."

I inspected the machine, worry creeping in around my appreciation for all the muscle and skin on display before me. The thing clearly had two sets of handles on it. "Is this a two-man job?"

"Not if one of the men is as strong as I am." He flexed for me, and I felt my eyes roll.

"I'm serious. Aren't there supposed to be two people operating this thing?"

He shrugged. "I can do it."

"What if you get hurt?"

Sly leaned in and ran his thumb over my cheek, capturing my jaw. "You worried about me, Clara?"

I stepped closer. "Actually, yes. Your livelihood depends on your physical health, doesn't it? And don't you have an exhibition game coming up?"

"Two weeks." Sly looked slightly less cocky, and then glared down at the augur. "Doesn't matter though. I'm not dragging Dad back out here."

"Of course not." I doubted Sam was supposed to be doing hard work out in the sun. "I'll help you." I had an hour before Katie would be done at school. "I just have to pick up Katie in an hour."

"Mom can do it."

"I couldn't possibly ask her. She's done so much already."

"Mom lives for that kid."

She did, I knew it was true. Violet had told me that she hoped my new job wouldn't mean I didn't need her anymore. I knew I'd find ways to include Violet in Katie's life either way. She was a wonderful role model.

"Let me just go put my stuff inside and put on some more sunscreen."

"You already worked all day. I can't ask you to—"

"You didn't ask. I offered, and you're not saying no. I can at least balance the other side for you."

Sly raised an eyebrow. "I mean, if you're looking for things to do for me, I can think of a few more than that."

I stepped close and kissed him quickly, a thrill spiking inside me that I could. We'd been flirting in stolen moments all week, and anticipation had been building for Saturday, when Katie would be at Betty's all night, and we'd have a solid block of alone time. "Tell me about them tomorrow."

Sly grinned as I turned to take my stuff inside, and when I got back out with a glass of sweet tea for him and my work gloves on, he was sitting in the shade of the maple that stood in the Remington's backyard.

I looked around as he accepted the glass and drank greedily, noticing a shiny new machine installed at the base of the garage stairs. "What's that?" I asked, pointing.

"I had air conditioning installed in the upstairs apartment over the garage. Upgraded Mom and Dad's too." He pointed to an identical machine next to the house.

"Do they spend much time up there?" I asked, gazing up at the garage apartment.

He shook his head. "That's my place. For now. All new furniture was delivered Wednesday, and I had the place scrubbed top to bottom. Just in case you, uh . . ."

I raised an eyebrow and crossed my arms. "What are you suggesting?"

Sly stood and pulled me roughly against his bare chest sending a thrill dancing through my limbs as I tilted my chin to smile up at him. "I'm suggesting that I wanted to have my own place just in case you ever wanted to sneak over and visit." I had a fleeting worry that Violet might see us, but then realized I didn't care. Hadn't she hinted thousands of times that she'd like to see me and Sly together? I'd always laughed it off. But maybe Violet knew something I didn't.

I slapped him on the chest. "C'mon. Let's get to work."

Before I could escape, Sly pulled me closer, kissing me gently while simultaneously using his strong arms to keep me right where he wanted me. I pretended to struggle, but in reality, every bone in my body was screaming that I was exactly where I'd always wanted to be. When he released me, I was breathless.

"Quit stalling, get to work," he teased, stepping over to pick up the augur from the ground. "Oh, by the way, I owe you a thank you."

"You do?"

"Yeah. We got an A on the project the second time."

"Yay! Congratulations!" I was relieved and happy for him. Relieved because I knew how hard he was on himself when he did anything less than he expected.

Sly's smile slipped a little, but he looked pleased with himself and I was glad. I stepped to take the second set of hand grips to steady the augur, and we got to work. I mostly made sure the big thing didn't topple over or put a hole where it wasn't supposed to while Sly manhandled it down the fence line, leaving holes big enough to sink posts into concrete.

Sly had convinced me to ask Violet to pick up Katie, and by the time she was skipping across the yard from the car, we were just finishing the last hole.

"Hey little bear!" I called.

"Mommy!" Katie wrapped her arms around me, and my heart soared as my eyes met Sly's. It felt like everything in my life had shifted gears in a very short time, and even though part of me was afraid to trust the happiness I felt, I didn't want to waste a second of it.

"What are you doing?" Katie's voice held a clear note of appreciation as she ran a hand over the hefty machine we'd laid on the ground. "This is so cool."

"It's an augur," Sly told her. "Digs big holes."

Katie continued to inspect the device and I tried not to be too obvious about my desperate attraction to the man who took everything she did in stride.

"Thank you for letting me pick up Katie once more, Clara," Violet said, crossing the lawn. "Oh my, you two have done a lot of work out here."

"Thanks so much. Sly did most of the work. I just made sure he didn't get hurt."

Violet beamed at me, then looked up at her son. "Dad didn't come back out?"

Sly shook his head and I could sense the worry pass between them. "Just tired, I think."

A tiny sigh escaped Violet before she offered me a sweet smile. "Will you and Katie stay for dinner? I made chili and cornbread, and there's way too much."

"Cornbread!" Katie cried happily. "Yes!"

I smiled at my neighbor. It would surprise no one to learn that I hadn't planned for dinner yet. "I think we'd love that. What can I bring?"

"Just yourselves," she said. "But give us a half hour. Sly needs to clean up." She wrinkled her nose as she took in Sly's sweat-soaked cap and glistening chest.

Whatever she saw was definitely different than what I was seeing, which was probably for the best.

"I do too," I agreed, feeling the sweat sticking the back of my T-shirt to me and matting my hair to my neck.

"See you soon," Violet said, turning and heading into the house.

"Good day?" Sly asked Katie.

"Mmm-hmm. Why are you digging holes?"

Sly patiently explained how he was going to build the fence, leading her down the line and explaining the whole process as she asked questions. I watched them, loving the way he was with her, the way she looked up so clearly to him. I found myself wishing for things to be so much more than they were, but cautioned my rollicking heart to take it slow. I still had no idea what this really was. Soon, Katie and I went inside so we could get cleaned up.

Sitting across the table from him at dinner was a sweet kind of torture, knowing that the next night we'd finally be alone. I wasn't sure what his parents knew, or what Katie had figured out. Not that there was much going on, not really. But I luxuriated in the newness of whatever it was, in the satisfaction of a years-old longing inside me. And the anticipation of what might happen the next night, when it was just the two of us, had me equal parts nervous and giddy.

I slept in on Saturday morning—as much as that was possible with Katie around. She tended to get up around six every day, regardless of anything at all. But that morning she came to my room, bringing at least sixteen stuffed animals and thirty-seven books with her, and she read quietly in my bed while I snoozed.

When I finally felt like it was time to wake up, I pulled her close to me and held her in my arms, snuggling in her little-girl sweetness as the sun brightened the shades on the windows.

"Happy Saturday, little bear," I whispered.

"Happy Saturday, Mommy." Katie wasn't often still, so I relished the times when she let me cuddle her, knowing that these days would vanish rapidly and I'd be left with a big kid determined to assert her independence, and I'd miss the little girl who thought I ran the world.

"Are you excited about your sleepover?" I was excited about mine.

She nodded against me, but then stiffened. "What if I don't like Betty's niece?"

"You like Betty, don't you?"

"I love Betty. She has blue hair."

"She does. She's also a lot of fun to hang out with. So if you like Betty, I'm sure you'll have fun, even if her niece isn't your favorite person."

"Well I already know she's not my favorite person."

"How do you know?"

"Because you are. And Silllvesterrrr is second." She was quiet for a moment as I smiled into her hair. "Oh wait," she added. "He is tied."

"With me?" I asked, a tiny bit hurt that he could waltz in here and tie with me in just a couple weeks' time.

"No, you're first. He's tied with Miss Violet."

"Aha. Yeah, that seems fair."

We spent the morning lounging while I pretended I wasn't watching Sly and his dad out the window as they poured concrete and sank the fence posts along the line between our houses. Sly was shirtless again, so it was impossible not to linger near the windows. It was almost a relief when we piled into the car and headed for the mall. I had it in my head that I might find a new sundress to wear to the barbecue, and had promised Katie a new pair of shoes.

By the time I'd dropped Katie with Betty and was showered and lotioned and clad in my new fitted red maxi dress waiting for Sly to ring my doorbell, I'd become decidedly nervous.

But the way Sly's eyes lit up as he took me in from head to toe told me that I wasn't wrong about what might happen tonight.

"You look incredible," he said, stepping close and wrapping an arm around my waist to lean in and kiss my cheek.

"Thank you." I admired him too. He wore a pair of dark jeans and a white short-sleeved button-down shirt in a light summery fabric. And flip flops. He looked like a movie star headed for his yacht, with his aviator shades perched atop his head in his perfectly waved dark hair.

"I never see you with your hair down," he said, sounding entranced as his fingers found a strand over my shoulder and touched it tentatively. "It's gorgeous."

"Thanks," I said, beginning to get a little uncomfortable in the face of his admiration. "Should we go?"

"I'm deciding if I really want to share you with my teammates."

I frowned at him. No one was sharing me. "Ew."

"That's not what I meant." He took my hand. "Come on, let's go."

I locked up and tucked myself into the passenger seat of his car as he stood holding the door open for me. He shut it gently and went around, sliding in and giving me another appreciative glance. He let out a low whistle and shook his head, and then started the engine and backed out.

I was nervous about meeting his teammates. I'd never been super comfortable with the athletic crowd, which always made me think of the popular kids in high school. Of Sly, really. Unattainable, perfect. But here he sat next to me, glancing at me constantly as if he couldn't get enough of me, and I had the sensation of being in a completely different version of my life. One where I wasn't the nerdy mathlete, one where I dated guys like Sly Remington, where I went to prom with them, where I was confident and secure and—

"What are you thinking? You have a funny look on your face." Sly grinned at me.

Caught. I cleared my throat. "Nothing. Just happy to be out. With you."

He reached over and snagged my hand, holding it between us on my seat. "Me too. Thanks for coming with me."

"You're welcome." The glow inside me emanated so strongly I was pretty sure it was showing as I smiled, but I didn't care. I was happy, for once. And I was going to enjoy every second of it.

CHAPTER 16
SLY

CRITICAL QUESTION: BIG OR
SMALL?

Was it crazy that I felt an outsized sense of pride as I walked into Stephano Mizzoni's backyard with Clara at my side? I'd felt a shade of the sensation before—the girls I dated were usually gorgeous, and generally made it clear to anyone watching that they thought I was attractive. Or maybe they just thought I was famous. And rich. And could therefore give them things . . . but it was no great feat convincing one of these women to join me at a team event.

The pride I felt now was matched with something else though, and maybe it related directly to why I'd dated those other girls. It was fear. The superficial women that dated me because of who I was didn't expect anything beyond what they saw on the surface. But Clara? I wasn't entirely sure why she was with me. What did she want from me? And why did I feel like I'd move heaven and earth if I could, just to give it to her?

"Sly!" Elks and Gillespie stood next to the barbecue, and greeted us as we rounded the garden path toward the extensive outdoor kitchen and deck next to Mizzoni's pool.

"Wow, this is really nice," Clara said, looking around.

I slid an arm around her waist as we stepped onto the deck. "Hey guys. I'd like to introduce you to Clara."

They stared at me for a beat too long, and I realized they were waiting for the rest of the introduction. Maybe for me to add, "my girlfriend." But that wasn't what this was. Not yet, anyway.

"Clara, nice to meet you," Gillespie said, stepping forward and giving Clara a kiss on the top of her outstretched hand. The guy was always weirdly formal, and there was some speculation that he'd descended from royalty or something, but he said he was from New Jersey, so it didn't seem likely.

"Glad you could make it," Freddy Elks told her. "It's really nice to meet you. I hope you won't hate us all after you see what we're really like."

Clara shook her head and laughed. "I don't have any preconceived notions about what any of you are like," she told him. "So I don't think I'll be disappointed."

Elks shot me a look like he couldn't believe I'd brought such a catch, and then returned his attention to her. "So what do you do with yourself when it's not hockey season, Clara?"

"Um, pretty much the same things I do when it is hockey season, I guess. When is hockey season?"

Elks and Gillespie shared a look of surprise, and then seemed to mutually decide Clara was telling a joke, and burst out laughing. Clara wrinkled her nose, adorably unsure what she'd said that was so funny. "No offense," she added quickly.

I shot them a hard look and pulled her away. "Let's get a drink."

Mizzoni's place had an entire bar outside next to the kitchen, where a couple of the other guys were already seated, in deep conversation about something.

"Sly," Tyler Cornwall said, turning to me as we approached. "Settle an argument for us."

I frowned at Corny and Simpson, who both looked too invested in whatever they were arguing about for anything good to come from me taking sides. "Just grabbing a drink, guys. Meet Clara."

"Hey," Cade Simpson said, shooting her a smile and a nod,

and then his face took on a serious expression and he said, "Clara, you help us decide. If you could be either really, really big or really teeny tiny, which one would you choose?"

Corny turned his attention to Clara, and I watched him give her the once-over, feeling my arm tighten instinctively around her waist as he did.

She laughed, a nervous melody, and then said, "well, I guess they'd each have challenges. How big is big? I mean . . . if you couldn't ride in a car or fit through doorways or into buildings, that'd be a pretty significant issue. But if you were super small, you'd be in danger all the time. Cats, dogs . . . getting stepped on. I don't know."

"Small is better," Corny said.

"No," Simpson argued. "Now we have to decide how big is big. And how small is small?"

Corny nodded while he sipped his beer. "You're right."

"We'll leave you to it. Let us know when you figure it out. Critically important," I said, ushering Clara to the other end of the bar, and then moving behind it to face her. "What can I get you?"

"This is pretty serious," she said, regarding the extensive line of alcohol bottles on display along the back wall.

"Mizzoni just moved in a while ago. He's a little particular, so we're no longer allowed inside the house."

Clara laughed. "Why? What'd you do to the house?"

"It wasn't me," I assured her. "But I think some of the guys might've gotten crumbs on the couch."

"That's awful," she said, barely covering her amusement.

"Making fun of me again?" Mizzoni appeared, stepping through the screen door and sliding it shut behind himself, a bowl of tortilla chips and guacamole in his hands.

"Of course not," I told him. "That's so much more fun to do when you're actually present to witness it."

He set the bowls on the bar top and wiped his hands on his shorts, turning to Clara.

"Hi, I'm Stephano."

"Clara," she said, shaking his hand.

"You're Sly's friend, huh?"

"We've known each other forever. Since high school," she said.

"Seems like you've had plenty of warning then," Mizzoni said. "I won't bother."

"Hey," I chimed in. "Be nice. I'm a delightful person."

Clara and Mizzoni both shot me skeptical looks, but Clara's slid quickly into a smile. "You are."

"Get you some drinks?" Mizzoni asked, joining me behind the bar and then making a shooing motion like he was trying to get a pesky fly to stop bugging him. I moved back to the other side of the bar and sat next to Clara.

"Margarita?" I suggested, spotting one in front of Gillespie at the other end of the bar.

"That sounds good," Clara said.

Mizzoni turned to the fancy machine whirring behind him and dispensed two margaritas for us.

"Be careful," I warned her. "Last time these had an extra kick."

"No worries, I've put a lock on the lid of the machine," Mizzoni said over his shoulder.

I laughed.

"Your yard is beautiful," Clara told him, turning on her stool to take in the huge structure that turned the patio into more of an outside living space than a yard, the sparkling pool shining in the late afternoon sun beyond. There were trees and hedges, a wide swath of lush green grass, and flowers blooming around the borders.

"Thank you. It's become a bit of a refuge." Mizzoni set drinks in front of us and lifted one for himself, holding it out for a toast. "Thanks for coming," he said, touching his glass to Clara's and then mine. "It's always nice to meet an old friend of a teammate."

I didn't like the term "friend" one little bit, but if that was what Clara was going with, I couldn't really argue.

"Tell us what Sly was like in high school," Corny suggested, sliding his chair over to sit on Clara's other side.

"Not necessary," I suggested.

Clara gave me a smile and then turned to look at Corny and Simpson. "First, what did you decide?" she asked.

"Bigger," Simpson declared.

"I'm still not sure," Corny told her.

"You can see my intellect fits right in with this crowd," I murmured into her ear. She frowned at me, and then swung back around to address my teammates.

"Sly has always been one of the nicest guys I know," she said. "I wasn't exactly popular in high school, and he was always kind to me, always friendly."

"You were popular, Sly?" Corny sounded like this was hard to believe, and I was about to decide whether to make him apologize when Clara spoke again.

"He was the most popular guy in school. Hockey star, prom king—"

"Friend to stray dogs and flightless birds," Simpson added, his hands over his heart.

"Shut it," I growled at him. "You too, Clara. You're ruining my image."

She laughed and Mizzoni leaned in. "What image do you imagine you're protecting?"

"I know you guys think I'm just this handsome and unknowable tower of masculinity and unmatched athletic prowess. I don't want her to ruin the mystery for you by humanizing me." I sipped my drink, chuckling as they all exploded into laughter.

"Right," Corny said. "Like there's anything we need to know beyond the fact that you're always exactly where you're supposed to be to make a shot. And that you'll beat the shit out of anyone who even looks at Mizzoni the wrong way."

There were murmurs of approval. I wasn't alone in that one. We protected our goalie like he was made of glass, but I'd seen Mizzoni hold his own in a fight too.

I tried not to let Corny's dismissive words rile me. Maybe I hadn't let all the guys see past the image I worked hard to protect, but it had never bothered me to hear it—until now.

"I think there's plenty below the surface," Clara said, taking my hand. My whole body warmed at her touch.

I watched as my teammates exchanged not-too-subtle glances.

"Awww, she's defending you, Sly." Simpson said, pushing his broad shoulders into Corny's personal space as he leaned forward. "That's actually really awesome." He grinned widely at us. Simpson's beard was huge and unruly, and Corny frowned as it came perilously close to dipping into his drink.

"Dude!" Corny pulled his glass away from the imposing beard.

"This is new," I told them, gesturing between Clara and me. "So no analysis is needed, thanks."

Simpson and his beard retreated back to the other end of the bar, and I could hear him posing another question to Corny that would undoubtedly have them debating for another hour or so. "Invisibility or the gift of flight?"

"Excuse me," Mizzoni said, picking up a cloth behind the bar and heading down to wipe up something in front of the guys at the other end.

For the first time since we'd arrived, Clara and I were left alone.

"A little overwhelming?" I asked her.

She shook her head and took a sip of her drink. "No, it's fun to meet your teammates. I guess this would be like me taking you to an office party."

"Do you have an office party coming up? Was that a subtle invitation?"

Clara's blue eyes twinkled. "I don't, but I would invite you if I did."

"Thank you. I would accept. Even if there were going to be bears in attendance." I wondered what Clara's coworkers would think of me. They were all scientists, like her . . . it would be a tough crowd to impress. I pushed the thought away.

We sat together for a little while, absorbing the increasingly rowdy banter around us as I enjoyed the feeling of being close to Clara, of having her at my side and knowing she was here with me. I saw the guys eyeing her appreciatively in a way I'd never seen them do when I'd brought other women to team events. A warm glow of pride lit inside me. She was here with me. She'd chosen me.

More people arrived, and soon there was an assortment of food spread across the long table, and everyone moved to pick up plates and find spots to eat. Clara and I carried our plates to the edge of the pool where there was a round table with an umbrella, Rock Stevens and his fiancée already settled and eating beneath it.

"Join you?" I asked them.

"Please," Drea said gesturing to the open seats. "I haven't gotten to meet you yet," she said to Clara. "I'm Drea. This is Rock."

They exchanged pleasantries, and once we were seated, Clara looked back at Drea. "We're literally the only two women here."

"There's a rule," Rock said around a chicken leg.

"A rule?" Clara asked.

"There's no rule. It's nothing," I suggested, a tiny prick of panic welling up in me. Clara did not need to know about the rule. "Rock, how's your shoulder? You ready for the game in a couple weeks?" Rock had been playing a lot of pickle ball and had evidently developed something he called "pickle shoulder," which the team doctors were a little worried about.

"Shoulder's fine. There is a rule," he said, waving the leg at me now. "It's new. And it's his fault. Not that it affects me."

Drea shook her head, as if they'd spoken previously about Rock's propensity for waving barbecued meat around.

"What's the rule?" Clara asked. "No women at team parties?" Her face wrinkled into adorable confusion, and I wanted to pick her up and carry her away before Rock told her why there were no other women here. His revelation would only serve to confirm to her the image I was working so hard to break away from.

"Only fiancées, wives, and serious pursuits allowed at team events." I winced. What would Clara think of being pushed into the category of 'serious pursuit'?

Clara appeared totally unfazed and looked around again. "None of these guys are married?"

Thank god that was the part she latched onto. "Houstein got married last year, but it's a long-distance thing. Girl in his hometown out in Oregon," Rock told her. "And Ackerman has a full-on family, but his wife hates us so she never comes."

"He's not here either," I pointed out.

"Because she thinks we're a bad influence on the kids," Rock went on. I actually thought kids would have a great time around us, and I knew from my own time with Katie that we could be civilized when needed.

"That's sad," Clara said.

"It is," Drea confirmed. "He seems pretty miserable, honestly."

"Anyhoo," Rock went on breezily as I cringed, "a certain someone liked to bring a particular breed of lady friend around and it usually caused some kind of shenanigans that were just not worth the trouble."

"What?" Clara laughed, and I could tell she had no idea what he meant. What would Clara think if he told her the whole truth? This wasn't something I really wanted to explain right now.

But Drea had clued in and was giving me a look of sympathy now.

"Yeah, Sly here—"

"Rock, do you want more chicken?" Drea cut him off, and I knew she was trying to save me.

"No thanks, babe. I'm good." He set down the chicken leg and wiped his hands. "Sly usually likes the simple ladies. The ones who date players for the money and the fame, and to get access to the team. He's famous for towing around scantily clad girls who aren't too loyal to one guy over another, and once you add some alcohol to that situation, things tend to go south." Leave it to Rock to paint the picture clearly in very few words.

Clara frowned at me. "I've seen a few photos, if I'm being honest, but I just figured you had a type."

"If he does," Rock said, heaping on the crap now, "I don't think you're it." He leaned forward. "And that should be a relief."

"That's probably enough," Drea suggested, dropping a hand on his back and shaking her head.

"I don't have a type," I said, realizing there wasn't much that would save me here. "I just like to keep things light."

"Oh yeah?" Clara said.

"I mean . . . it was just easier. Before."

"Before what?" she asked.

I shot a look at Rock, and Drea stood, handing him his plate. It occurred to me that I would have done better calling the actual team shrink. Rock did not practice doctor-client privilege. "We're going to go check out the dessert options. So nice meeting you, Clara."

"You too," Clara said, and then turned back to me.

When they were gone, I put down my fork and faced her. She didn't look angry or upset, just curious. "I don't have a type, exactly. I just try to stay uninvolved, if that makes sense."

"Is that what you're doing with me?" Her tone was light, but the words were loaded.

"No." The word came out fast, almost harsh, and I chuckled, rubbing a hand across the back of my neck. "I mean, I kind of wish I could. But you already know way too much."

"What do you mean?" Clara was leaning in close, and I could smell the soft vanilla of her skin, the clean scent of her hair.

"You know everything," I admitted. "All the stuff I try to keep hidden around these guys."

"Like school?" she asked.

"Yeah. The fact that this is literally all I have. Hockey. It's all I've ever been good at, all anyone cares about when it comes to me. So it makes sense that the women I've dated have been really invested in that. In me as a hockey player and nothing else." As I spoke the words, I realized how shallow it sounded.

"You do know you're a lot more than that, right?" Clara was so close to me now, this was a whisper. "You can't really believe there's nothing more to you."

"I want to think there is."

"Would I be here if there wasn't?"

My lips brushed hers, and I wished suddenly that we were alone, and that I could just pull her into my lap and continue this conversation without words.

"Sly." She pulled back and gave me a stern look. "If all there was to you was hockey and this"—she waved her hands over my chest—"body, these looks . . ."

"You like my looks?" I grinned at her, happy to lighten the mood for a moment.

"You know you're hot. But what we both know is that there is a hell of a lot more to you. The way you love your family so much that you're living in a garage apartment all summer to keep an eye on your dad and help with stuff around the house. The way you take care of Katie, and tolerate fingernail polish and tea parties. The way you look out for me . . ." She trailed off and looked up into my eyes, and I had the uncomfortable sense that she could see deeply inside me to everything I kept from the world.

"And your motivation and drive," she went on. "Not just for your sport, but to be something more. To better yourself. To use your not-insignificant intellect to ensure you have a path when hockey ends." Her hand was on my cheek now, and I leaned into the soft touch.

"Sly, you're so much more than the looks or the sport. And that is why I'm here." She leaned in close and kissed me for real, and every cell inside me vibrated in an effort to get closer to her, to seek out more of the warmth, acceptance, and validation she offered.

Shit, I was in trouble.

"Thanks," I said after she pulled away, leaning my forehead against hers. "That's really nice to hear."

"Do you think we should go soon?" she asked.

I moved away so I could get a better look at her. Was she tired of me now that I'd shown her my insecurity? But no. The look on her face wasn't one that said, "I'm ready to go home now, jerkwad." It was a whole lot closer to the look I imagined was probably on my own face. One that said something like, "let's go check out your new bed together."

"Yeah?" I asked. "My place?"

"You said you'd had the place furnished . . . I'd love to see it. Last time I was up there to help Violet with something it was full of boxes and dust."

"Let's say our goodbyes."

Five minutes later we were back in my car, and my heart was racing as I thought about what the rest of the night might hold.

CHAPTER 17

CLARA
THE VIP TOUR

Seeing Sly with his teammates had been enlightening in a strange way. On one hand, it was clear how close they were, that they had each other's backs, that the men were as much brothers as they were teammates. But then, on the other hand, it was also clear that Sly had never really let his teammates see the whole of him. He'd never given them the chance to know and support the real Sylvester. He was playing a role, and it made me sad.

But as Sly parked his car and came around to open the door for me, I didn't feel sad at all. I was experiencing a wide set of sensations—from some kind of bizarre high school do-over feeling to a thrumming excitement moving through me. Was this really happening?

"I feel like we're sneaking around," I whispered, as Sly ushered me down the long driveway past his parents' place and up the back stairway on the garage.

"I mean, we can go in and say hi if you want." He did not sound in the least like this was what he wanted.

"No," I laughed. "It's okay. It's just bizarre. We could go to my house." The offer was half-hearted. I wanted to go to Sly's place, knowing he'd fixed it up with me in mind.

Sly unlocked the door and reached inside to flick on the lights before tugging my hand and pulling me inside. He shut the door and then caged me against it, his broad chest and strong arms holding me there so that all I could see, smell, or think about was him. "What's bizarre?" he asked. "You and me?"

I stared up into the molten brown chocolate eyes that had been part of my dreams for as long as I could remember, and my body tightened in anticipation. "Yeah, a little bit."

"Do you want to go to your house?" he asked.

"Not really," I admitted. Being away from my regular life, away from reminders of Katie and the fact that I was a mom made it easier to fall into the fantasy of Sly Remington.

"That stuff you said . . ." Sly was looking into my face like it held secrets that would determine the fate of the world, or his, maybe. "About the way I was in high school. Did you really feel that way?"

"Of course I did. So did anyone who knew you. I still do."

He let out a sound that was part growl, part exhalation, and stepped back, capturing my hand as he did so. "Let me give you the tour."

We didn't have to go anywhere for the tour. I could see the entirety of the small apartment—minus the bathroom—from where I stood at the front door. But it had changed a lot. Where the place had been nothing more than storage for as long as I could remember, now it was a sleek, well-appointed studio apartment.

One end of the space held a king-sized bed standing beneath the window looking out over the garage. To one side of that were two doorways, the closet and the bathroom, I guessed. The front door opened directly into a living area that held a leather couch and coffee table, and a side chair upholstered in a soft gray fabric. An enormous television hung on one wall, and there was a kitchenette tucked into a little bump out in the far wall with a refrigerator, stove, oven, and sink. A little island stood to one side and a small round table with two chairs completed the space. The floors shone as if they'd been recently scrubbed, and the walls had clearly been painted, and were hung with prints that looked like French ads for alcohol from the twenties.

"I love it," I said, looking around appreciatively. "You did all this just to be here for a couple months?"

"I did it for Mom and Dad. They can use this as a guest space, or Mom might make it her craft space. I wanted to do it nicely so they'd be proud of it."

"You're a good son," I said, meaning it. If I hadn't already been attracted to Sly, that would have tipped me over the edge.

"You haven't even seen the whole thing," Sly said, pulling me into the center of the space.

"I'm not sure what else there could be," I laughed. "It's not that big!"

"No guy wants to hear a lady say that," Sly said, tugging me up against his chest and putting his arms around me.

"Not what I meant," I managed, though the proximity of Sly's hard body pressed against mine made words harder to come by.

"Did you see the bedroom?" Sly asked.

"I think so."

"The VIP tour includes a test drive of my new bed."

"Then I guess I'd like the VIP tour, please." Even as I said the words, the surreality of the whole situation struck me. What I wouldn't have given all those years ago to be in this exact spot, in this man's arms . . . But before I could lose myself to the wistful nostalgia, Sly's hands found my waist, and he spun me so my back was to the bed, and then picked me up and gently set me atop the deep grey comforter.

"I'll just get these for you." He knelt at my feet and took one of my calves between his big palms, pulling my foot to rest on his massive thigh. And then he carefully unfastened the tiny buckle on my sandal, sliding the shoe gently from my foot before repeating the process on the other foot.

There was something so sweet about the action, and I wanted him more than ever. It was like I was the only one allowed to see this side of him, the real Sylvester Remington. And I wanted to see it all.

"Come here," I suggested, scooting back on the wide bed.

Sly stepped out of his flip flops and crawled up the bed until he reached me, and then straddled me, placing one knee on either side of mine and smiling down at me where I rested against the soft pillows at the head of his bed.

"I like having you on my bed," he said, his eyes deep and sensual.

"What will you do with me, now that you have me here?"

Those eyes darkened, his lids dropping slightly. "I have a few ideas," he said. And then he leaned down and took my mouth with his, tossing me right back into the land of fantasies fulfilled.

For what felt like hours, we kissed, our bodies intertwining against the soft cushion of Sly's big bed. We rolled one way, then another, and there was such an unhurried and languorous quality to the time he spent exploring my body with his hands and my mouth with his tongue, that I began to wonder if he was planning anything else, or if maybe this was the extent of the VIP tour.

But then he rolled me to my tummy, and straddled me from behind.

"Are you about to give me a back rub?" I asked, trying not to be disappointed.

"No," he said. "Unless that's what you want. But I've spent the last half hour trying to stealthily unzip this goddamn dress, and I can't fucking figure it out. I needed to put eyes on this chastity lock you've got here."

I laughed into the mattress. "It's just a hook and eye at the top."

"Designed by someone who did not realize that if you wear a sundress this sexy, it needs to come off fast." He managed the zipper then, tugging it down my back. He slipped the straps from my shoulders and moved down my body as he eased the dress down and off. I heard his own zipper, and the sound of his jeans hitting the floor.

I was about to roll back over, when Sly's big hand landed on my calf.

"Now this is a nice view," he said, and my face heated, but there was no way he could see it. I could sense his gaze traveling over my legs, my ass, my back, and a moment later, his hands were on me. They traveled up the backs of my legs, hot and huge, leaving a trail of shivery goosebumps in their wake. He paused to palm my ass for a long second, and then climbed over me again, but this time, the warmth of his naked flesh slid against mine, sending spirals of lust twirling through me.

As he slid up my body, trailing kisses up my spine and finally gently moving my hair to one side and covering my neck with kisses, I felt the hard steel of him against me. When his firm thickness landed in the seam of my ass, I groaned at the same time he did. And when he began to move, gently rubbing himself there as his hands and mouth had their way with me, frustration began to bubble inside me. He had me pinned, and I could do nothing but lie there, accepting his attentions, when all I wanted was to wrap myself around him, to feel him in the center of my want before I melted into a withering pile of unfulfilled flesh on his new bed.

I struggled, trying to flip myself over.

"Not yet," he murmured, and his hand slid beneath me, caressing my stomach as his breath washed hot over my ear. His palm moved down my stomach, slipping into the silk of my panties, and as his mouth teased my earlobe, his long fingers found my pulsing desperate center and I let out a relieved moan.

"You're sopping wet," he whispered, sounding pleased.

"Because you're torturing me," I groaned, still desperate to touch him, to feel him against my chest.

"Is this so bad?" he asked, working my clit with his expert fingers as his hard erection pressed into my ass. It was a heady sensation, I was surrounded by him completely, unable to do anything except experience exactly what he was giving me.

He pressed his fingers into me, urging me to lift my hips, arching my back to give him better access, and we both groaned as he slid a finger into me, his palm grinding into my mound as his shaft thrust against my ass. It was so erotic and so different from anything I'd experienced with a partner before, I finally gave up and lost myself to the sensation. He was in me, around me, over me. His hands, his big body holding me to the bed, and his hot breath in my ear, against my neck.

Sly moved rhythmically, and I found myself grinding into his hand, spreading my legs slightly to give him more access, desperate for more, for everything.

"Oh god," I groaned, still so needy, wanting so much more.

Sly leaned in to capture my mouth again, and it was such a relief to have him there, to be able to participate, to kiss him back, I almost cried. I felt like I might explode.

Finally, he moved off of me, and my body mourned the loss of the contact. But not for long. I rolled to my back, and Sly reached for the nightstand, pulling a condom from the drawer.

"You okay with this?" he asked.

I stared at him, on his knees next to me on the bed, completely naked. His erection jutted before him, held in one huge hand, and throbbing visibly, the head swollen and dark. He was beautiful.

"Yeah," I said, pulling my panties off and kicking them to the side.

I watched in fascination as Sly rolled the condom over his massive length.

And then he was back, stretching himself along the side of me, and offering me a soft smile before he took my mouth gently with his own, his hand splayed across my belly.

Finally, my hands were free to touch, to explore, and I traced the broad expanse of his chest, sprinkled with soft hair. I moved over the hard mountains of his shoulders, traced the bulges of his muscled arms, and lingered along the ridges of his back. He kissed me all the while, his fingers teasing lower and lower along my stomach before finally returning to my wet folds.

I gasped as he grazed my clit, working it with one talented

finger until I was clenching muscles I didn't even know I could control.

I reached for him, finding the sheathed thickness with one hand and guiding him toward me.

"I need this," I moaned, and it was truer than it had ever been. He'd taken a perfectly put-together single mother and turned her into a needy, wanton woman, desperate for one thing only. And that thing was hard and thick and throbbing in my hand. I gave it a squeeze as I tilted my hips to accommodate the wide head, and groaned as it pushed inside gently, filling every bit of space.

"Fuck," he breathed into my ear, his body covering mine again.

My hands slid to his ass, pulling as if I could urge him inside, asking him for more.

I felt myself opening for him, my hips lifting, my legs wrapping him. Sly didn't let up the pressure, easing in slowly, bit by bit. I was so wet, it made it easy, and after a moment, I was so full with him I could hardly form a thought.

"Oh my god," I heard myself breathe, but my mind wasn't engaged. My body was so full of Sly Remington, every nerve wrapped up in the sheer sensation of him, of holding him inside me, of having him on top of me, his breath in my ear, his stubble against my cheek, I was lost to anything else. And when he began to move, sliding gently out before thrusting slowly back in, I let out a sound I wasn't even sure came from me.

It was so good.

I lost myself completely to it, to him. And Sly played my body like it was made for him, like I was the instrument and he was the prodigy who'd spent his life training for this moment.

The pressure was mounting inside me, and desperation rocketed through me. "Please," I moaned. "Sly. Please."

"I've got you," he whispered, tightening his hold on me as my body gripped his tighter and tighter, until finally everything in me unlocked in an explosion of heat and want and sensation that sent me flying.

I had no idea what kinds of sounds were coming from me, only that I didn't want it to end.

"Oh my god," I moaned as I began to float back into my body. I'd never orgasmed like this before, in a way that made me feel like my entire being was carried away in the sensation, like every single part of me was involved.

But it wasn't over.

Sly had kept the exact same rhythm as I'd come undone, but now that he was sure I was sated, he'd shifted slightly, and now he was driving into me hard, and my body started to respond again to this new, different motion.

"Fuck," Sly whispered. "That was so fucking hot." He thrust into me, again and again, and I could sense the change when he began to lose control, the pattern altering slightly, a shiver passing through him. "Oh god, I'm gonna . . ." And then his whole body tensed just before he thrust again, with a pulsing need that told me he was coming. Feeling him come apart was such a turn on, my own body responded. Again.

"Oh . . ." I gripped him hard and felt the wave wash through me, less intense this time, but still overwhelming.

CHAPTER 18
SLY

DEATH BY SMOOSH

As I rose from the depths of a crazy dream where Mizzoni was singing opera while Gillespie and Simpson skated around the rink with Rock on their shoulders in a tiara, I took stock.

"Morning," Clara said watching me from where she lay curled up just inches from me.

We were in my bed, curled up facing one another like little kids at a sleepover. It was a lot different from the way we'd spent most of the night, tangled together, lost in each other's bodies and breaths. I pushed a lock of glimmering hair off Clara's forehead, my heart surging at the way she looked with her fist pushed up under her chin, those blue eyes staring into mine.

"Good morning," I said, and felt the lazy grin slide across my face.

Clara just smiled at me, and I wished I could see what she was thinking, but I was a tiny bit afraid to ask. Had I been snoring? Did I fart? Why was she smiling at me like that?

"I never get to sleep in," she said, her dark eyelashes lowering and rising again like lush little fans. "This is so nice."

"So are you using me for my quiet bedroom?"

"Among other things," she said, her voice lowering into a sexy purr.

I reached a hand out, dropping it onto the curve of her hip and tugging her closer so our noses were just inches apart. "Oh yeah?"

"Yeah, the air conditioning in here is pretty good too."

I frowned at her.

"And these sheets are nice. What's the thread count, four kajillion?"

I grunted a warning.

"I like this pillow too. Very supportive."

I pounced, pulling her close as I rolled on top of her, trapping her beneath me as she squealed and laughed.

"Be nice or I will smoosh you."

"Do not smoosh me. You're enormous. I'll die in seconds."

"Then you might want to rethink all the things you're using me for." I lowered my weight a fraction and she squealed again.

"Fine! I'm using you for your humongous cock and your magical fingers, and that thing you do with your tongue!"

"Better." I rolled to the side and pulled her on top of me.

"And to get closer to the Wilcox Wombats, of course. Now I've got all the juicy details. Who knew your goalie was such a clean freak?"

I laughed. "Mizzoni? He's just a little grumpy."

"You have a grumpy goalie. That sounds like a good title for a book!" She giggled, and I leaned in close to kiss her.

"You don't even know when hockey season is," I pointed out. "You don't care about getting the inside scoop on the team."

"I only care about one hockey player," she said, and my heart beat a little faster. I kissed her again.

"Want to take advantage of me some more? I don't have anywhere to be today . . ."

"You don't," she said, sounding disappointed, "but I have to pick up Katie by ten."

I glanced at the clock. "It's only nine."

"I will need to be wearing clothes and not smell like sex."

"Hmph. Do you want to smell like breakfast?"

"I mean . . . depending on what's on offer." Many inappropriate offers flew through my mind, but I settled on actual breakfast options.

"You hop in the shower. I'll make pancakes."

"Coffee?" she said hopefully.

"Yup. And strawberries and whipped cream." As I said it I wished I'd thought to offer that last night. There were a lot of uses for whipped cream.

"Okay," she said, sitting up. But then she glanced around and frowned. "I should really go home, though."

"Why? You don't think my shower will live up to high standard established by the thread count? There are three shower heads in there, sweetheart."

She giggled. "It's more about clean underwear."

"I have some shorts and a T-shirt you can throw on until you get home."

She looked up into my eyes, considering. "Walk of shame in your clothes."

"The only people who might see you are my parents." Which would result in far more questions for me than for her.

"Makes it so much better."

I kissed her then, and I felt her resistance melt away. "Pancakes," I whispered in her ear, forcefully pushing myself to let her get up. Trapping her here wouldn't help either of us, no matter how much I wanted to.

"You really know how to get a girl worked up." She poked me in the chest and scooted off the bed, and I had to fight down the urge to tackle her naked body back into the sheets. She was so damned hot, all muscles and sinew paired with luscious curves in exactly the right places.

I handed her a pair of workout shorts and a Wombats T-shirt, and sent her off to the shower. Then I got to work.

When Clara headed down the stairs after pancakes, refusing my offers to walk her home, I didn't want to let her go. I wanted to stay curled up together in the little cocoon we'd created. I had a crazy thought that as long as we stayed up there together, we could keep things exactly the way they were—perfect. As long as I was holding her close and looking into those gorgeous eyes, as long as I was listening to her breathy moans and making her laugh, this was our whole world.

But our world was bigger than just us two.

And it involved children, and teammates, MBAs, and parents.

And a fence that wasn't going to build itself.

I pulled on shorts and a ball cap, slathered on some sunscreen —because sunscreen is important—and headed down to the backyard to work. Now that the posts were sunk, the rest of the fence was simple enough to construct. Dad had helped put up the crossbeams, but screwing the planks on seemed to be up to me. I could hear the television blaring inside. Today it sounded like bowling.

Go figure.

As I picked up the first plank from the pile and readied the electric screwdriver, Mom called out to me from the back porch.

"Sylvester, honey."

I turned to face her, not sure if she needed to chat. She sat in one of the oversized patio chairs, a cup of coffee in her hand and the paper on the table in front of her. I put the plank down and headed over to say good morning.

"Hey Mom."

"Sit down for a minute and talk."

"You doing okay?" I asked, taking in the half-finished crossword and her slightly drawn expression.

"I am. I can't hear myself think in there with the television going all the time."

I raised an eyebrow, thinking about that. "You could ask him to turn it down."

Mom sighed and one shoulder lifted and fell, like it would just be too much to ask.

"Did you and Clara have a nice night?"

I'd mentioned that I was taking Clara to the team barbecue,

but now I wondered if Mom had sat here quietly and watched Clara leave my place this morning.

"We did," I said, trying not to give anything away. I didn't want to embarrass the woman I couldn't stop thinking about.

"And you were a gentleman, I expect?"

If a gentleman makes a woman come screaming his name at least four times in one night, then I was a perfect gentleman. "Of course."

"She deserves some happiness," Mom said, and I had the sense she was talking about more than Clara. Mom was staring off into space, looking more resigned than I'd ever seen her.

"Mom, what's going on?" There'd been something funny about the way she and Dad had been interacting since I'd gotten home. He was getting away with a lot more than usual. It wasn't like Mom to play the submissive housewife.

"Mmm?" she shook her head lightly, her lips pursing.

"With Dad. Here."

She held my gaze for a moment and then dropped her eyes to the table, tracing an invisible line across the surface of the newspaper with her finger.

"There's obviously something wrong," I prodded. Now that I was asking, I was connecting all the dots. I hadn't been sure before, but now I was convinced there was something going on.

She nodded, but didn't speak.

I waited, my heart freezing inside my chest with every moment she made me wait.

"I guess it's his heart?" Mom said quietly.

"What do you mean 'you guess'?"

"Dad had a little heart attack a couple months ago," she said, still not meeting my eyes, probably because she knew there'd be an inferno there. How could they not tell me?

"What?" My voice was a low whisper.

"Something about the valve in there . . . but he has a new one now."

I shook my head. "Dad had heart surgery? And you didn't tell me?" I stood, needing some kind of outlet for the anger surging through me. I wanted to pound something or someone to let out the sudden burst of adrenaline inside me.

"It was the beginning of playoffs. We didn't want to worry you. Dad said it would throw you off your game."

"Did Beckett know?"

Mom didn't answer.

I paced a circle around the little deck. "So my whole family kept a huge secret from me because you thought I couldn't handle it. Dad could have died. And what would you have told me then?" I was speaking a little louder than I meant to, but I hadn't yet made sense of the fury zinging around within me.

"He's okay, honey. He's just supposed to take it easy, is all."

I stared at her. "You didn't think I could handle this information now? When I'm living here for the summer? When I've been forcing him out into the hot sun to work on this fence with me?" Guilt compounded my anger over the way I'd cajoled Dad outside, pushing every macho button I knew he had. I could have killed him!

"I'm sorry, honey."

I nodded because I didn't trust myself to speak. And then, when no appropriate words came to me, I turned and headed for the stairs.

Once inside my apartment, I paced some more, willing some kind of understanding to sift through the hurt and anger ricocheting around inside me.

Finally, I came to a stop in front of the window looking out our backyard. And Clara's.

Katie was there, turning in circles on their grass and then throwing herself down dramatically and laughing. I could barely hear the tinkle of her crystal laughter from here, and it settled something inside me. I stood there for at least ten minutes, just watching her get up over and over, laughing all the while. And my anger eased.

I pulled a bottle of water from the fridge and sat down on the couch.

Why hadn't they told me?

Did they really think I couldn't handle it? Did they think that hockey was so goddamn important to me that I wouldn't want to be there for my family?

I chugged the bottle as an unwanted realization dawned.

They didn't tell me because they knew hockey was all I had. They didn't want to do anything that might jeopardize the only thing I was good at, the only thing that kept me afloat in this life.

I slammed the bottle down and dropped my head into my hands.

Even my family believed I was nothing more than a jock.

I glanced to the little table where my books were piled for school. I had one more year ahead of me. One more year of hiding my true self, of pretending I was happy with everyone assuming I was an idiot. One more year of suspecting they were all right. And then what? I'd have some outside validation that I was, in fact, worth something more?

Fury spun up in me again and I wasn't sure where it was coming from or what to do with it, but I suddenly realized that I didn't want to prove anything to anyone. What was I busting my butt for? Even my own mother thought I was too one-dimensional to handle anything besides the smacking of a puck down the ice or the pounding of some other dumb jock into the wall. Why was I working so hard to prove them wrong? It wasn't going to make a difference anyway.

I stood, crushed the bottle and went back into the yard to build the damned fence.

CHAPTER 19

CLARA
YAHTZEE

I didn't see Sly again that weekend, except in quiet moments when I closed my eyes, reliving the night I spent in his apartment over the garage. If I laid very still and slowed my breath until it was nearly absent, my mind could almost recreate the sensations I'd experienced when he was near. I could conjure his hands on me, his hot breath on my neck, the sense that in his arms I was exactly where I fit best.

But it had been so quiet since then.

We exchanged texts here and there, and the week was busy as I began my new responsibilities at work and Sly went to the rink each day to work out ahead of the exhibition game.

I missed him. Which was stupid. It's not like I'd had time to get used to him in the first place. And he was temporary in my life at best.

That's what I kept telling myself.

I was getting home at regular hours now, and Violet met me at the door each afternoon when I arrived to pick up Katie. School was out, so Katie was staying next door all day. I'd planned to send her to camp, but Violet wouldn't hear of it. Most nights, I found myself with time to make a proper dinner, and by

Thursday night, I was even indulging in some weeknight socialization.

"Tell me everything," Andie said, holding the wine I'd just handed her and seating herself at the kitchen table as I continued chopping vegetables for the salad. "The girls are watching a movie. They can't hear anything."

Andie's daughter Stella and Katie were as close as Andie and I were, thanks partially to the fact we were pregnant at the same time, both suffering less than ideal marital situations. The girls were snuggled up with the couch cushions on the floor beneath a blanket in front of the TV, watching one of the four thousand Ice Age movies.

"Like . . . tell you what?" I asked her, though I was pretty sure exactly what she wanted to know about my one night out with my high school crush.

"Well, when he first came back and you had that dinner next door, you told me you hated him. Now you're spending the night?"

I glanced at Katie, but she was giggling merrily with her friend. "Things were weird when we first met again. We just needed to clear a few things up."

"Like . . . what?"

"Like . . . I don't know. He didn't seem impressed about my job."

"Literally everyone on earth is impressed when they find out about your job. You're stinking brilliant."

Andie had always been my champion. I lifted my wine glass to her. "Thanks, Mom."

"It's true. What's his issue?"

"No, I don't think he really has one. He just thought maybe not being out in the field made more sense since I've got Katie to think about."

"So completely not the call of the high school hottie you haven't seen in a decade." She shook her head in disgust. I thought about the way he'd celebrated the promotion, but it hadn't felt like anything but happiness on my behalf by then.

"True, but I don't think that's really an issue. Plus, I'm not in the field now." I finished the salad and put the chicken in the oven to bake. "Back deck?"

She nodded, glancing once more at our daughters with their adorable heads together on the pillows in front of the movie.

As we stepped outside, my gaze went automatically to the half-finished fence between my house and Sly's parents' place. And to the stairs leading to the apartment over the garage.

"Uh huh." Andie followed my gaze. "Okay, now. Spill it. What happened?"

We sat and I took a deep breath, trying to push down the giddiness that threatened to turn my voice into a high-pitched, high-school shadow. "He took me to a team barbecue at the goalie's house."

"You met Stephano Mizzoni?"

I gave her a skeptical wide-eyed stare. "You're a hockey fan suddenly? I mean, I met the whole team. Or a lot of them."

She gave a non-committal wave of her hand. "I wouldn't call myself a fan, exactly. Just . . . I like to watch now and then. Especially Mizzoni. And it's fun to say I went to high school with Sly Remington."

"You've literally never mentioned this."

"Because Sly has always been kind of a loaded subject." She took a sip of her wine, her big dark eyes watching me warily as if I might explode or burst into tears. When I calmly sipped my wine, she went on. "So tell me everything about Saturday."

I put down my glass and leaned forward, trying to collect my feelings into a bundle that I could easily sort through. "It was good." That was a completely inadequate beginning. Before Andie could protest, which her mouth dropped open to do, I went on. "We left the party right after dinner and went back to his place."

"To hang out with his parents?"

I shook my head slowly, giving her my best just-you-wait look, and pointed to the garage apartment.

She followed my gesture. "He lives up there?"

"He had the whole place cleaned up and furnished."

"Bet it's nice with the hockey money to spend." She wiggled her eyebrows and I was glad there was enough distance between my deck and the garage that Sly couldn't hear us whispering if his windows were open.

"I mean . . . they were the softest sheets I've ever rolled around in."

"Shut up!" Andie literally leapt out of her chair and then sat back down and lowered her voice. "You rolled around in his sheets? Was he like, in the bathroom or something?"

I shook my head slowly, grinning. "He was right there."

"You mean you had—" The girls chose that inopportune moment to appear on the back patio. Andie cleared her throat and leaned back in her chair. "You played Yahtzee with Sly Remington?" This was delivered in a stage whisper that immediately attracted the attention of two curious little girls.

"What is Yahtzee?" Stella asked, her dark eyes on her mother's face.

"Are you talking about Siiiiilllllvesssssster?" Katie pretty much yelled this.

I glanced at Sly's open window in time to see his face appear as the shades were pushed aside. My heart flitted around in my chest, and a second later, my phone dinged with a text.

Sly: Talking about me?

So much for the thought that he couldn't hear us. I could feel the blush climb my cheeks.

Me: Katie is.

Andie was watching all this with a half-smile of amusement on her face.

"Mooommmy?" Stella still wanted to know what Yahtzee was.

"It's a game, honey. With dice."

Sly: And you? By the way, is that Andie?

Me: You remember her?

Sly: Of course. Tell her hi for me.

"Sly says hi," I told her, unable to suppress the smile I was beaming down at the phone in my hand.

She spun around and stared at the window, where Sly lifted a hand to wave.

"Mom, it's Siiiilvessster. Is he coming over? Are you going to play Pot-see again?" Katie danced in front of me, waving madly at Sly.

"No," I told her. "It's girls' night. And no Yahtzee tonight."

"I want to play Yahtzee with him." Katie stuck out her bottom lip, but she didn't pout long because Stella grabbed her arm and pulled her out onto the grass where they both started spinning. I wasn't sure why spinning was Katie's current favorite activity, but I figured it was better than sitting in front of the television, so as long as she didn't crash into anything and give herself a concussion, I wasn't saying anything.

Me: Everyone says hi.

Sly: You ladies have a good night.

I put my phone down but picked it up when it chimed again almost immediately.

Sly: Up for a late-night visit?

I should say no. Katie was home. But Katie went to bed before nine and if I was very lucky, she slept like the dead.

Me: Okay.

Sly sent a little thumbs up sign, and I dropped my phone, doing my best to suppress the goofy smile that I could feel on my face.

"Okay, you better start talking. Clearly this was not a one-game situation with the Yahtzee and whatnot," Andie said in a much quieter voice.

"I wasn't really sure at the time. But yeah, I think it's not a one-game thing." We were both whispering now.

"So?" she asked, rolling one hand in front of her in a go-on motion. "Is he good with his dice? What are his cup-shaking skills like? Did you get a Yahtzee?"

"You know an awful lot about a kind of ancient dice game."

"Stop stalling."

"I Yahtzeed. Four times."

"Holy cheese balls!" Andie cried, fanning herself. "And the equipment?" She glanced at the girls and lowered her voice again. "Was the table of an adequate size for all that dice rolling?"

"The table was huge."

"Fuck." She whispered it under her breath, but we both glanced at the little girls spinning on the grass, oblivious to our discussion of Yahtzee. "I really want to play some Yahtzee with someone that has an adequate table."

I nodded. Andie was separated, and I knew things had been rough for her lately. "I want that for you too. It was amazing."

"And so? There will be more games?"

I took a deep breath and let it out. "I don't know, really. He's staying with his parents for the summer, and I was helping him with—" I cut myself short of telling Andie about his MBA. "Some things."

"That's very mysterious."

"Sorry, I promised I wouldn't tell."

"Now you're definitely telling me."

I never kept secrets from Andie. And I was pretty sure she didn't have anyone to tell. I lowered my voice even more. "He's getting a graduate degree, so he's taking online classes. And I just helped a bit with some data stuff."

"Sly Remington is in graduate school?" The smile was big enough to worry me.

"It's a secret," I reminded her with a finger to my lips.

"Why? Is he afraid it'll ruin his jock image?"

"Maybe. I don't know. Maybe he doesn't want people to think he's not fully committed to the team?"

She put a finger to her mouth, considering. "I guess that makes sense . . . Something weird about it, though. Still, I really care more about your ongoing Yahtzee tournament. There will be more rounds?"

"He asked if he should come over tonight."

"Oooh." Andie smiled and a dreamy look passed across her face. "Should we take off?"

"No. You're having dinner with us! Besides, there's no Yahtzee until after bedtime."

"Right."

"When's dinner?" Katie called from where she lay on her back in the grass.

"Right now," I called back. "Come help set the table please."

We headed in for dinner then, Andie and I doing our best not to discuss dice games too much in front of the kids, and the evening concluding with a long hug on my front steps.

"Thanks for having us," Andie said. "I'm glad you got the new job. You seem more relaxed. But maybe that's just all the dice . . ."

I sighed. I wanted to tell her that the new job was amazing and better than being in the field. But it just wasn't. "Maybe. It is definitely easier knowing what every day will look like."

"You don't sound thrilled."

"I guess it's just . . . less fun than being in the field."

"Well, it's only day four. Maybe it gets better."

"I expect it will. I ordered some new sticky notes that might come in tomorrow."

"Oooh," Andie laughed. "Bright colors?"

I nodded, "Of course."

"Well, I'm sure that'll fix everything."

Katie and Stella hugged goodbye and promised to see each other soon, and my daughter and I watched as they headed off into the dim glow of the summer evening.

"Time for bed," I told Katie, ushering her back inside.

She protested, because that was her job, but soon she was bathed and tucked in, stories had been read, and lights were out. I tried to push down the giddy excitement bubbling in my stomach as I picked up my phone to text Sly.

Me: If you'd still like to pop by, Katie just went
to bed.

Sly: Should I wait a bit? Be sure she's asleep?

I didn't want to wait. I wanted to play Yahtzee. Now.

Me: Fifteen minutes. If I keep things quiet right after she goes to bed, she's a good sleeper.

Sly: Why does no one ever praise me for that? I'm a fucking fantastic sleeper.

I laughed quietly.

Me: I meant to tell you that Sunday morning. That I was really impressed by your sleeping prowess.

Sly: I think you were impressed by other things . . .

I waited, but nothing else came through, so I busied myself brushing my hair and teeth and nervously tidying the house.

It was almost nine when a quiet knock came at the door, and I let out a nervous giggle, rushing over to open it.

Sly stood on my doorstep smiling. His dark hair was tousled and the smile revealed dimples far back in his cheeks, giving him a jovial innocence that made me want to jump him. He had on low-slung dark jeans and a soft-looking green T-shirt, and he was standing close enough that whatever scent seemed to cling to him

— leather and mint (dirty candy if you listened to Katie) — teased my senses.

"Hi," I said, suddenly shy.

He looked me up and down, slowly, like a wolf eyeballing a sheep it was about to eat, and a shiver went through me unbidden.

"Hi," he said, his voice low and warm. "Katie asleep?"

"As far as I know. Come in."

I moved back and Sly stepped inside, shutting the door behind him.

We stared at each other for a long moment, and then the moment snapped and I was in his arms, his mouth devouring mine hungrily. I kissed him back, every bit as hungry, my hands sliding up beneath that soft shirt and reveling in the feel of his hot, smooth skin.

Sly's hands were as insistent as his tongue and lips, sliding, gripping, exploring. And then he pulled back and before I could prepare myself or register what he was about to do, he leaned in and literally swept me off my feet, carrying me back to my bedroom and setting me gently on the bed before turning back to quietly shut and lock the door.

"I would have kicked it shut, but . . ."

"Glad you didn't."

He faced me then, his eyes ripping every shred of clothing from my body and devouring me. My skin heated beneath his gaze, and the distant desire I'd had for him all week boiled into a desperate need.

"Come here," I pleaded.

"I'm coming," he said. "Just wanted a second to look at you, to remind myself how lucky I am."

"You'll get a lot luckier if you're over here," I pointed out.

He laughed, and it broke a bit of the thrumming tension I felt. And then he joined me on the bed, stretching out beside me and pulling me close.

"I mean it," he said. "How lucky I feel that you'd want to

spend time with me. Like this. Or at all, actually."

I was tracing his strong scratchy jaw with my fingers, but I stopped and met his gaze, finding a shadow there that hadn't been there before.

"Why would you say that?"

He opened his mouth to say something, but then seemed to change his mind, and the words that came next didn't match his cloudy expression. "Because you're incredible, Clara. You're so ridiculously smart. It's just . . . "He broke off and leaned in, his lips slanting over mine and ending the conversation. I wanted to ask another question, but my brain slowly began misfiring as Sly's hands on my body stole my power of speech.

He undressed me slowly, covering each inch of newly exposed skin with his mouth, tracing patterns with his fingers, leaving little trails of shivers everywhere he went. By the time I was naked beneath him, a shivering needy pile of woman, I'd forgotten the conversation, abandoned it completely in exchange for what I knew was on the horizon.

I was going to Yahtzee again. Soon.

Once I'd wrangled Sly out of his clothes, I pushed him to his back and climbed over him, wanting to appreciate the view of this hot, hulking man sprawled out naked in my bed.

It was true I'd been married to Katie's dad, and I had loved him. But sex with Zach was never like this. With him it felt like something to be done in the dark, handled and then moved on from. It felt sneaky and a little bit shameful even.

This, with Sly, felt more like a destination to be explored, enjoyed. It was the difference between buying a Hershey's bar at the grocery store and eating in the car on the way home, feeling guilty about it and picking up a box of gourmet chocolates at some fancy boutique, setting them brazenly on the counter and then savoring them one by one in front of anyone who pleased to watch.

I traced long lines around the prominent muscles of Sly's chest and abdomen, loving the way his eyes glistened up at me full of appreciation and something that looked a whole lot like wonder. I followed my fingers with my mouth, trailing kisses and nips down his stomach and across his hips, finally letting one hand slide down to graze the steely soft length of the erection.

He sucked in a breath when I touched him, and when I grasped him firmly, stroking him up and down, he let out a low groan that pulled at something deep inside me, ratcheting up my want exponentially.

I slid lower down his body, cupping his balls in my other hand as I pumped him, adding my tongue to the mix with a long swipe up the underside of him. Sly's hands found my hair, burying themselves in it as I finally took him into my mouth, sealing my lips around him and sucking gently, following my hand up and down as I stroked him.

"Shit," he murmured. "That's good."

His grumble had an edge of hysteria to it, like he was on the brink of losing control, and the knowledge made me feel powerful in a way I wasn't sure I had before.

I continued my work for a few more minutes, reveling in the way Sly tensed and moaned beneath me, and when his hands moved to my shoulders and tugged, urging me back up his strong body, I complied.

"Condom?" I asked him. I had some—I'd bought them this week on the way home, hoping exactly this situation might arise, but I still felt a bit shy. I didn't want him to think I'd expected this to happen again.

"In my jeans," he said, gesturing to one side of the bed.

I rolled off him, but I could feel his hungry eyes on my skin as I reached for his pants, finding a string of condoms folded into his front pocket. I held them up, five of them dangling from my hand. "Awfully ambitious."

"You never know," he answered.

I ripped one off, opened it and rolled it down his length while pinching the tip to leave a little extra room. And then I leaned forward and kissed him again, Sly's arms banding around me like iron, and his body tensing beneath me. Still connected to his mouth, I reached between us, positioning him right where I needed him, and then slowly, I pushed onto him, our kiss never breaking as I took him in, centimeter by slow, delicious centimeter.

I was so ready for him that the sensation alone—that slick, satisfying slide—had me on the brink of exploding, but I held back. I didn't want this to be over.

Putting a bit of space between our bodies, I started to undulate my hips, playing with different rhythms and speeds, moving in various ways and watching Sly's reaction. He was so expressive, so open. I could tell exactly what he liked best by the way his eyes fluttered, the way his body tensed, and the sounds he made. Some people liked to listen to whale sounds, I thought absently, but I would be happy to have a soundtrack of Sly's sex sounds to listen to when he wasn't here. They ranged from soft grunts to strings of desperately muttered curses, and every syllable lit me on fire.

I tightened the muscles inside me deliberately as I pulled myself backward, letting go slightly as I slid back down, clamping again as our bodies met.

"What the fuck are you doing to me?" he asked, his voice low, his eyes glassy. His hands were planted firmly on my ass. I felt like I'd taken some kind of mind-altering substance, like I was floating above us, watching as he filled me so completely, his fingers brushing the sensitive spot between my cheeks as I moved. It was the single hottest thing I'd ever experienced.

Tension coiled inside me as I watched him fight for control. "You like that?" I asked, already certain of the answer.

"I don't know if I can form actual words," he said, sucking in a shuddering breath as I slid almost completely off of him and then slammed myself back down. "Oh fuck."

I was finding my pace, driven by my own need, and I increased the rhythm slightly, earning a groan from Sly.

Sweat rolled down my back as I moved, working toward a release I knew would be so big I was almost afraid.

When it came, on the heels of everything inside me tightening, it was in crashing waves of pleasure so intense they were incapacitating. I heard myself crying out, a breathy sound I didn't recognize that seemed to be coming from far, far away.

And as soon as the waves began to subside, leaving me limp, Sly took over the rhythm I'd set, holding my hips with his hands as he thrust up beneath me.

"Holy. Fuck. You're. So. Fucking. Hot." His words were punctuated by his movements, and when he neared the end of his statement, his eyes widened and his grip on my hips became almost painful, his fingers sinking deep into my flesh as he came.

He was quiet, which I was thankful for since I didn't want to have to explain this particular version of Yahtzee to Katie right now. But part of me would have liked to hear him roar his release, to know that I did that to him, that I brought that out of him.

We lay connected for a long time after, me resting on Sly's strong chest, his arms around me, one hand toying with my hair at my shoulder. Finally, I slid to one side of him, releasing him, and went to clean up. When I returned, he had snuggled down into my blankets and smiled at me.

"I don't think you can stay," I said, but I wished he could.

"I won't. I just want to hold you a little longer. We haven't talked all week."

I climbed in beside him, snuggling close and breathing in the heady scent of him, mingled with the lingering smell of sex.

"How was your week?" he asked.

"Good, I guess."

"A rave review."

I chuckled. "I guess I'm just going to take a while to adjust to being in an office all the time."

"It's what you wanted, right?"

I nodded against him. "Yeah. It's better for Katie."

"Better for you, too, right? More money, more responsibility?"

I sighed and Sly tilted his chin down to meet my gaze. "If you don't like it, don't do it."

"It's not that easy. I accepted a promotion."

"So?"

I thought about what he was saying, but I knew it wouldn't go over well at work if I changed my mind. Everyone else who was a contender had been told they didn't get it. They'd have to start the search again if I bailed. "I thought you didn't like me out in the field anyway."

"I don't. Wrestling bears doesn't seem like the right thing for you to be doing when you've got Katie here to worry about. Or me."

"I should be worrying about you?"

"No, but if one of those bears puts a paw out of line, they'd have to worry about me for damn sure."

"Thanks for offering to beat up a bear for me. Very chivalrous." I chuckled against him. It was nice to hear him offer to protect me, but it still irked me that he didn't see that how much I loved my job trumped any perceived dangers in my mind. My former job, at least.

"I don't like this job for you either though," he said, and it immediately rubbed me the wrong way. It was like Zach all over again, the only way he'd be happy about my work was if it was completely benign.

"Kind of not about you though," I said.

"Yeah, you're right. I'm sorry."

I relaxed against him again, determined not to let the irritation I felt ruin what we'd just shared. "How was your week?"

"Not great," he said bluntly.

I arched up to get a look at his face. "Why?"

He sighed, and I moved away a little, supporting my head on my hand so we could see each other. "My dad had a heart attack this year," he said.

I nodded. "I know."

Sly sat up abruptly, and then turned to face me, his expression murderous. "You knew?"

"I was here when the ambulance came," I said. "Did

you . . . did you not know that?" Why wouldn't his mother have told him? Wouldn't she have called him when it happened?

"No. No one mentioned it to me." Sly's face was dark, storms raging in his deep brown eyes. There was something more here, but he wasn't telling me what it was. "Didn't want to distract me during the season," he said, nearly spitting this last part.

"I guess that was considerate. They were thinking of you." I couldn't believe Violet would keep this from him, but didn't feel like it was my place to say so.

"You think so?" This was an accusation, not a question.

"Hey." I lifted both my hands in surrender, facing him on the bed. "I don't have anything to do with this. I don't know why they didn't tell you. I'm sorry."

He stared at me, hard, for another beat. And then I saw the fight flow out of him. "Not on you." He slumped, bowing his head and resting his forearms on his legs, which were bent beneath the covers. I moved closer and dropped a hand on his back, smoothing the long muscles there.

"Hey. You okay?"

"Yeah. I'm fine." He swung his legs out of bed, and I watched as he dressed, feeling like something had shifted but I didn't understand exactly what.

Sly peered over his shoulder at me. "You and Katie are coming to the game next weekend?"

I nodded.

"And the wedding?"

I nodded again. "Zara asked Katie to be the flower girl."

Sly sighed and turned to face me, seeming to push away whatever had chilled the space around him. "Good," he said, his voice warm again. "I know my mom kind of already asked you," he said. "But will you go with me? Be my date to the wedding?"

The desperate teenager who still lived inside me dramatically shrieked and threw herself, giddy, on the bed. Sly Remington had basically just asked me to the prom.

"Of course."

CHAPTER 20

SLY

IS A QUILL BOAR BASICALLY A PORCUPINE?

Monday, I headed up to Wilcox and spent the week in my own apartment, making it easier to practice with the team ahead of the match. It was also easier to be away from my family, and even from Clara, so I could focus. I was keen to get my head right to meet the Quill Boars on the ice.

It might have been just an exhibition game, but that didn't mean it didn't matter.

It was nice being back in my quiet apartment, except it gave me a lot of time to think. But what I really needed to do was study.

There were two things keeping me from buckling down on classwork: Dad and Clara.

Things had been tense with my parents when I'd called. Dad was his usual self, which is to say that I didn't speak with him because he was watching some game or another from his chair when I called. It wasn't like I usually called home a lot, but I guess I thought maybe I'd catch Dad, maybe he'd decided to tell me himself about his health. Or that maybe Mom had mentioned she'd told me and he'd want to talk about it. Clearly, not the case.

"Are you ready for the game, Sylvester?" Mom had asked over the phone the night before. I hated the note of desperation I heard there, like she knew she'd done something wrong and I was the jerk holding a grudge about it.

"Yep." I didn't want to talk about hockey. It almost felt like if I did, I was just reinforcing her belief that it was all that mattered to me. Or that it was all I could handle discussing. I pictured myself screaming down the phone at my parents that I was an adult, that I could handle real-life issues just like Beckett could. For fuck's sake, he was my little brother. Shouldn't I be the one they came to with their concerns and worries as they aged?

Of course Clara knew.

That was a fact I hadn't quite figured out how to reconcile. She was close with Mom, I knew that. And hell, she was right there every day, and I was a couple hours away, seemingly too absorbed or too single minded to be bothered with things like whatever life-threatening health issues my parents might have.

"We'll see you there, son." Dad had told me this as I'd hung up the night before the game.

"Yep. See you there."

The dressing room before the game was the place I finally started to feel like myself again. The comforting routine of getting suited up, hearing my teammates banter. That was what I'd needed.

"Sly, is Clara here?" Rock asked this as he adjusted his pads next to me.

"I think so. Why?"

"No why. Just glad she's coming. Happy to see you happy."

I turned to him and glared. "I look happy to you?"

"No man, you look seriously pissed right now, but I figured that was just your game face." He stopped what he was doing and gave me his full attention. "Everything okay?"

"Yeah. No. I mean . . . there's just a lot going on."

"I think Hasselbeck is here." The team shrink. Whatever Rock saw on my face told him this one was out of his league.

I shook my head. "I'll give her a call later."

He shrugged and soon we were heading out to face the goddamn Quill Boars, and my mind shifted to its most reliable state. Hockey. Winning. Doing what I did best.

Stepping out on the ice was like coming home—the smell of the rink, the roar of the crowd. The Wilcox fans were screaming, and there were way more of them than of the Quill Boar fans. I scanned the seats, looking for Clara, but didn't find her. And as Rock stepped up for the face off, I pulled my attention totally to the ice.

As we got close to the end of the first period, two goals behind, I'd spotted Mom and Dad sitting with Beck and Zara up in the stands, but Clara wasn't with them.

Where was she?

"Get your head in the game," Deck growled as he shot past me after a whistle, seeing me scanning for her.

"That's a nice helmet, does it come in men's too?" One of the Boars players, Clint Hayes, asked, slamming me as I shot for Simpson.

"Was that a hit?" I asked him. "It's not Little League, Clint." Man, I hated that guy.

When the period ended, I was actually happy to leave the ice. Deck wasn't wrong. My head was all over the place. The Boars were up by two, and their most irritating player, Hayes, had been talking trash non-stop, chirping incessantly. Asking for it.

"I'm sending you back out, but you better show me some fucking focus," Coach Merit told me as the crowd took their feet for the second period.

"Got it," I promised him. As I headed out, I told myself I wasn't going to look for Clara anymore. Maybe she hadn't come, only she'd assured me she would. What if something had happened to her? Or to Katie? No. I didn't have time to worry. I had to shove her from my mind. My life had been just fine before

I'd gotten involved with the girl next door. It had been easy. Safe. No one was too involved in my business, no one made me question my place in the world.

Which was here, on the ice.

"Watch it!" Hayes elbowed me as he flew by, and I spun, fury clouding my vision.

"I am watching it," I told him, getting in his face. "And I guess they were right when they told me you were the worst player on your last team too."

I spun around him, closing in on the net as Gillespie drove toward me. I was open enough, and the shot was forming in my mind. That was my gift. I could see the way things would unfold on the ice, I could anticipate the movement, be exactly where I needed to be.

Only fucking Hayes was in the way.

The puck came my way and I turned, sending it hard at the net. The goalie dove, but I saw the opportunity. And then saw it hit the pole and rebound. Guys scrambled for the puck, but the action was out of my control now.

Fuck.

"Just like your mom," Hayes chirped in my ear. "Smoking pole like a champ."

That did it. My vision blurred, and my gloves were off before I even planned to jump the guy. Seconds later, the rink was a melee, fans screaming and my teammates shouting. I ripped off my helmet, not even considering the consequences. When Hayes was on the ground, The ref pulled me off, his voice deadly calm in my ear.

"Misconduct. You're out of here."

My vision tunneled, and I headed for the dressing room, ignoring the continued shouts of my teammates as Hayes's team called for retribution.

Once I was undressed, I sat, staring at the floor between my feet.

What the hell had I done? It was a fucking exhibition game, for god's sake. I tried not to think about my mom. I could picture her face. She'd never gotten used to the idea of fighting being part of the game, and I actually tried to abstain, as much as that was practical.

I could hear the roar of the crowd, and felt myself swirling down into an eddy of darkness. I was fucking everything up.

I showered, trying to drown it all out, forget everything. If my family wasn't here, I'd have considered just leaving, dealing with Merit and the team later. But I'd have to face my family. So I stepped out of the water and dried off, picking up my phone.

Clara had texted. My heart leapt into my throat, worry for her and Katie overshadowing my self-pity for a moment as I read the texts.

> Clara: Hey, we were a little late, sorry. See you after! Good luck!

And then, from just a few minutes ago.

> Clara: Hey. Katie's scared that you're hurt. If you have a chance, can you text to let us know you're okay? The fight scared her.

I dropped the phone. My heart was doing unfamiliar things inside me. I'd made Katie worry, and for that I felt awful. And knowing they were both here, that they'd seen me deck Hayes . . .

How had I gotten into this situation? Why should a five-year-old's fears matter to me?

Goddamit, I wasn't a family guy. I was a hockey player. That was it. And I'd managed to screw that up now because I'd let my head get into a completely different place than it belonged.

We ended up winning the game, and I took the beating the coach offered, along with the disappointment of my teammates. I deserved every word of it. By the time I was heading out to the restaurant where Mom had suggested we meet after the game, I was feeling more defeated than I could remember feeling before. I was heading down the wrong path. And the only thing I could see that had changed was this situation with Clara. That, and confirmation that my family didn't think I could handle being a contributing member. I was just there for entertainment, apparently.

I stepped into Tecate, the Mexican restaurant a lot of the fans hit after local games. Julius Ramon was at the bar, nursing a beer. I gave him a quick salute. The guy had been driving the Zamboni as long as I'd been with the Wombats. And he had a weird way about him. Like he knew shit.

I did not especially like the disappointed look he was giving me now, as I headed for the end of the restaurant where my family sat in a booth. With Clara and Katie.

Fuck.

"Silly! You're okay!" Katie spotted me and came bolting through the restaurant, flinging herself into my arms.

I picked her up, cursing myself for taking comfort in her little arms around my neck, her soft scent filling my head. I didn't deserve any of it. "I'm fine, Katie."

"That other guy hit you! I saw him." She pulled back to stare at my face, and then rubbed a hand down my cheek. My heart crumbled inside my chest.

"I hit him first, Katie. And I shouldn't have."

She didn't say anything and I realized my whole family was watching us, waiting for me to join them. "Let's go eat, okay?"

She nodded, but I sensed that she was disappointed in me too. I turned to head to the table, but someone stepped in front of me.

"Remi?"

Oh shit. Jason. From my MBA cohort.

I shook my head, hoping maybe he'd just disappear, that this wouldn't actually happen. I only turned my camera on when it was an absolute requirement, and then I wore a hat pulled low over my eyes. A Wombats cap. I was such an idiot.

"It is you. Hey man! Oh, shit . . . you're . . ." I watched him put it all together. "You're Sly Remington!"

Katie was watching all this in fascination as I held her on my hip. "I call him Silly because his name is Sillllvesterrrrr."

Jason grinned. "Hey man, wow, that's so awesome. Rough game," he said, shaking his head.

"Yeah. Well, I'll see you in class," I told him, sidling away from him. I didn't want to be rude to a fan, but this was a whole other thing.

"Okay," he said, still sounding a little overeager about the whole thing. "See you later."

"That was weird," Katie said.

I put her down as we got to the table. Everyone's eyes were on me, and I felt like the pressure was literally pushing me into the ground.

"Hey guys. Thanks for coming. Sorry for the . . . well, sorry." I slid in next to Clara, since that was the only open spot at the table.

"Hey," she said softly. My heart ripped apart a bit more inside me.

"Hi." I couldn't meet her eyes.

"Your team won," Dad commented.

"Yeah."

"Wasn't sure if you knew since you missed more than half the game," he said.

I nodded, dropping my eyes to my lap. "Yeah."

"That was my first hockey game," Zara said, clearly trying to break the tension sizzling around the table.

"Looked like it was Sly's too," Beck quipped.

"Shut it, saucemonkey."

"Sauce monkey!" Katie laughed.

I couldn't use any of the words I'd wanted to, given her presence.

"It was my first hockey game too," Katie told Zara. "I was going to be a hockey player like Silly, but now I think I will just be a tow truck driver. I don't want to have to beat people up."

"Oh yeah?" Zara asked, clearly charmed.

The conversation went on around me, and I did my best to be present, but my mind was twisting in circles around things I couldn't control, things I'd already screwed up. And Clara's hand had found my thigh and was resting there, in a reassuring touch I didn't deserve.

Finally, the meal ended, and we all went our separate ways. I wanted to linger here in Wilcox, to stew in my own misery, in my own apartment. But as she'd hugged me after I'd walked her and Katie to their car, Clara had said, "come over later maybe?"

And though I knew I didn't deserve her, though I knew I should just say no and tell her we couldn't go on like this, I heard myself say, "okay."

I would see her, tell her in person that I wasn't in a good place, that I needed to get back to focusing on hockey, on the one thing that I knew was there for me. And maybe see if I could pull my studies back together. There was no room in my life for Clara and Katie, for these enormous and confusing emotions I had now.

But all I wanted was to lose myself in her soft body, her warm bed, just one more time.

CHAPTER 21
CLARA
STUPID LOVE

Something was wrong.

Sly arrived an hour after I got home. Katie was exhausted, partially from her concern over Sly and everything that had happened after the game. Which was mostly that he'd been a completely different person.

Gone was the engaged, silly, funny guy who'd pulled Katie (and me) into his orbit and charmed us until neither of us had any choice but to fall in love with him. In his place was a guy that emanated darkness and some kind of deep disappointment.

Was it just about the game? In the end, his team won. I would think that would serve to make him happy in some way, though his own performance was probably something he wasn't proud about. I wondered what the guy had said to him to make Sly lose control like that. It was a little scary to see him lose control like that.

"Hey," said the hulking and handsome man on my doorstep. He didn't meet my eye.

"Hey," I said, trying to make my voice soft, reassuring. I realized it was the voice I used with drugged-up mama bears when I helped collar and tag them for tracking. But that was how Sly seemed now, hurt. Vulnerable. Needing me to assure him that I wasn't going to hurt him while he was down. "Come in."

He stepped inside and looked around, as if he was seeing my house for the first time. The old couch, the worn table where I'd eaten all my childhood dinners. I hadn't changed anything. My parents had died and I'd stepped right back into my childhood home. Not that Sly spent much time here when we were young.

"Beer?" he asked hopefully.

I offered him a smile, willing to do just about anything to make things the way they'd been before between us. "Sure. Let's go out back."

We headed through the kitchen to the back patio, each of us holding a bottle of beer. I'd pulled up the screens, since the mosquitos had come out in full force lately, and though the night air was warm, it wasn't the sweltering oppression we got during the day.

We sank into my deck chairs, side by side.

"So," I said, hoping he'd pick up on the question.

"Shitty day," he said, as if we'd just come to some kind of agreement.

"Tell me why."

"You were there."

"There's something else going on."

Sly's eyes met mine then, full of something that looked an awfully lot like hurt. But he didn't speak, just tilted the beer to his lips and then settled back into the chair, staring out into the darkness of my yard.

"You've almost finished the fence," I said, figuring a shift in topic was the right move.

"Yep. So I'll be out of your hair soon."

I tried to subdue the shock of his easy statement. "Right. Back to Wilcox, I guess?"

"Back to my real life."

I nodded, lifting my beer to my lips and thinking about this. I'd known we were temporary, that this was just a fling, but still . . . hearing him so easily cast whatever we were into the past was hard. "And me and Katie?"

I hated the vulnerability in my own voice, but I needed to hear him say it. It wasn't going to be easy to explain this to Katie.

"You can go back to your lives, I guess. You don't need any of my bullshit anyway."

"Your bull—" I shook my head. "Sly . . ."

"Come here," he whispered.

I turned to him. His dark eyes glowed in the dim light the open kitchen door cast on the patio, and the sweltering heat added to the surreal quality of the entire situation. He reached for me, his hand extending like a man reaching for some kind of salvation but not actually believing it might come. I fought with myself. I shouldn't go to him. Not like this.

But I did.

I took his hand, setting my beer down on the patio and reaching to swing the kitchen door shut all the way, killing the light that had been spilling over us. And then I slid onto his lap, my knees finding their way to either side of his thighs.

And some stupid misguided part of me believed that this was a chance to change his mind. One final opportunity to prove that we were worth keeping.

Our lips met, but nothing about the way Sly kissed me told me that this was anything but goodbye. There was a desperate finality to every swipe of his lips, every teasing touch of his tongue. His hands dug into my hips, pulling me into him with all the command and dominance I'd used to think he'd display in any sexual encounter. Before I knew better. Before I'd been touched by the tender and sweet side of my high school crush.

And I didn't care. That's how desperate I was for him. How much I wanted one more night with Sly Remington. Because even though I knew I was letting him go, I wasn't ready. Not yet.

He pushed my shirt over my head, and reached around me to release my bra, palming my breasts as I arched into him. His mouth found one nipple as his fingers played with the other, and I writhed on his lap, forgetting myself completely in the moment. I slid to the ground, easing his shorts off his hips, and dropping my own as I stood back up, letting my panties slide to the ground with them. And then I slid back onto his lap, our centers connecting and stealing my breath.

I knew we needed a condom. Sly was famously promiscuous and I was a mother, for fuck's sake. But part of me believed that if I interrupted whatever this was to ask, that he'd simply leave. And it would be over.

Instead, I swallowed the question and slid onto him, murmuring, "I'm clean. And I'm on the pill," hoping for some kind of similar statement from him.

"Tested. Clean," he grunted, his fingers digging into my ass. So I had that, at least.

I moved over him, feeling like he needed this, needed me, and reveling in the feeling of helping him with whatever it was that had him drowning suddenly in darkness. I wanted to save him.

Because I was stupid.

But more than that, because I loved him.

I'd loved Sly Remington since the first time I saw him next door when I was in ninth grade and his family moved into the house adjacent to mine. I'd loved him when I'd sat across the table from him all those nights, helping him with math, and desperately hoping he might notice that I'd done my hair a little differently, that I'd worn a darker shade of lipstick.

I was in love with him that one fateful night when prom had been approaching and he'd walked me to my front door after a tutoring session. When I'd gathered my courage and said, "Hey, I wondered if you were going to prom this year."

Of course he was. He was a senior. He was a god. And I was . . . why was I asking?

He'd grinned down at me, cocky and glorious even then, all that wavy dark hair falling over his forehead. "Might," he'd laughed. "Probably, I guess." Then he'd cocked his head and met my eyes in a way he'd never done before. He'd dropped his gaze to my lips and for the briefest moment, I'd thought just maybe, maybe he might kiss me, choose me.

I'd risen on my tiptoes, dropped a hand onto his bicep, hoping, waiting.

And then he'd straightened up and looked away. "Okay, well. I guess I'll see you there if you go, right?" And he'd turned and walked away, leaving me humiliated. What had I been thinking?

And now, was it just more of the same? I was moving over him, his cock filling me and sending me into a realm of ecstasy I'd never known existed . . . and as I gazed down into his face, I could see that he wasn't even here. Not with me.

"Where are you?" I whispered.

The glorious dark eyes squeezed shut. "I'm sorry, Clara."

I froze. What was happening?

"I just . . ." He tensed, and then I felt him relax, bowing his head so it rested against my chest. "Fuck," he growled, his hands digging again into my hips as he began thrusting up into me, harder now. "Fuck," he said again, sounding like he was in actual pain.

But I'd already tipped over the edge, and was spiraling back down the other side. Only, this time, I was alone there. It wasn't the same fulfilling togetherness we'd had every other time. It was rote. Physical.

Sly was getting himself off, and I let him. And when he finished, I climbed off and pulled my shorts back on, feeling embarrassed now. Even a little bit used.

"Well," I said, suddenly eager for him to go. To leave me alone to try to understand what had happened, how everything had changed so quickly.

"Yeah. Okay," he said, standing. "I'll see you later."

He kissed my cheek then, and let himself out the patio door, heading across the dark lawn to his own yard. I watched as his dark shadow headed up the stairs to his apartment.

And then I went inside and cried.

CHAPTER 22
SLY

I finished the fence the next morning, beginning work at six-thirty and putting away my tools by noon. The neighbors probably didn't appreciate it, but I didn't find that I cared much. There was one neighbor I did care about, but she was the reason I needed to go. And then I packed my bags and left, giving my parents vague excuses about team obligations and hockey.

Those were the only ones they'd probably believe anyway. Or the only ones they wanted to hear.

I needed to get everything back the way it was before I'd come here, before I'd fallen in the trap of trying to relive high school but do it better this time. I was me. Why would I believe doing it as an adult would somehow create different results? I lived in a box created by my own talent for one single thing. And a smart man would get comfortable in there, and realize it was enough.

But that was my whole entire problem. I had a sinking feeling that now that I'd seen outside the box, what was inside it would never satisfy me.

I got back on the ice every morning with a few guys from the team, and hit the gym every afternoon. I kept my body tired enough that my mind didn't try to take over.

Which made it pretty fucking hard to study.

I'd only signed on for school twice since I'd bumped into Jason in the restaurant, and my suspicions were confirmed. He'd told my entire cohort exactly who I was.

I got a B in Data Visualization and then emailed the administrator to let him know I was putting the rest of the program on pause. Who knew if I'd ever pick it up again? It'd been a stupid idea in the first place.

"Dude," Mizzoni pulled me aside one morning, two weeks after I'd gotten home. "We're having breakfast."

I shook my head, focusing on tying my sneakers and not meeting his gaze. I'd been skating with the team, working with my teammates to get ready for the season. But I hadn't really been here, and I knew it. "I ate."

"I don't care." Mizzoni's voice lowered to the threatening whirr of a saw's blade. "You're coming."

I glanced up at him, and found the same look he gave Gillespie when the guy had accidentally broken one of Mizzoni's pool chairs. It was dark and glowery, the kind of gaze I thought serial killers had probably perfected.

"Fine," I said, not really wanting to go, but not wanting whatever weird confrontation Mizzoni was gearing up for either.

Twenty minutes later I sat across from him at the Toasted Toast, a poorly named breakfast joint slash karaoke bar near the arena. It was a far less painful destination for breakfast than it was for a drink, at least.

We sat in silence as Mizzoni appeared to read every single entry on the menu, despite having been here at least four thousand times like the rest of us. When he'd considered every option and we'd finally ordered, I sat there staring into the dark, slightly oily top of my coffee, doing my best to pretend I was alone. Mizzoni made that easy by not speaking.

Finally, he put down his own coffee cup with a thud and let out a long exhale. "You're going to be a really good disappointed dad," I told him, finally looking up to meet his disgruntled gaze.

"I'm not disappointed, I'm just angry."

"Take back what I said. You got that completely backward."

"What the hell is going on with you?"

"These are the jokes, man. All I've got." I knew he wanted more, but I wasn't sure I wanted to spill my guts right here on the table over toast.

"Not with your stupid jokes. Nothing's changed there. With your head." Mizzoni's face was dark and he held my eyes with his penetrating gaze, making me feel almost pinned down. A reporter had written once that half the goals he saved were thanks to the way he looked at anyone who got close to our net.

"I'm trying a new mousse," I said, lifting one hand to my hair, which I hadn't bothered getting trimmed lately. I knew it looked like shit. I also knew he wasn't asking about my hair.

He slowly shook his head back and forth, an action that became somewhat less threatening when the waitress deposited a stack of their "frooty booty" waffles in front of him, covered in whipped cream, berries, and rainbow sprinkles.

My own poached eggs on avocado toast looked naked in comparison, but I couldn't eat all that sugar after a workout. Though it might be worth it for the spectacularly vibrant vomit it would certainly produce. "You must have a gut of steel."

"Not important. Talk about Clara."

Her name was like a knife in my gut. "You met her. She's a scientist. Has a kid. Lives next door to my parents."

"And?"

"Um . . . very bossy, poor driver. What else?"

"Feelings."

"You're really good at this deep talk stuff."

"I'm trying. You need a friend." Mizzoni shoved a forkful of waffles into his mouth and I let that sink in. The guy was stoic and reserved all the time. But for him, this was an enormous and uncharacteristic gesture of friendship.

My resolve started to crack a bit. I sighed, letting my shoulders relax a little. I was exhausted, though I couldn't pinpoint exactly why.

"I'm okay, man, I promise," I told him.

He watched me for a long moment, those dark eyes calculating. "I don't think you are. You're serious, which is not normal. And you've got a new aura. Darker. Fuzzy."

I nearly choked on the bite I had swallowed as he said this. "Say what?"

He didn't answer, just stared at me.

"Say what you said again. You see auras? Around people? Like colors and stuff?"

He nodded. "Always have."

"Are you into crystals and tie dye too?"

"Don't stereotype me. Various gifts run in my family."

"Spooky."

"I'm an empath."

"You're the grumpiest empath I've ever met."

"Why do you think I'm so grumpy? I spend all day trying to stay out of other people's issues, and it's fucking exhausting."

That actually did make sense. "And me?"

"I'm worried about you, and whatever this is, it's not getting better. I think it's Clara."

The absence of Clara and Katie from my daily life had left a bigger hole than I wanted to acknowledge. My cold, stark condo was a constant reminder of the life I'd chosen for myself, of the person I was. And it was so empty it hurt. But I had hockey, and that would have to be enough.

"Your game is a mess," he went on, his tone never shifting.

"My game is on point." That was the one thing I was sure of.

He shook his head. "You used to play with a kind of finesse. It's what makes you so great. Unpredictable. Like you already know you're going to score." He paused to run a finger through the whipped cream on his plate and stuff it into his mouth. "Now? It's like you're trying to force it." That seemed annoyingly accurate.

"What color was my aura before?'

"Glittery pink."

"Shut up."

"It was."

"You're just fucking with me now." I had the aura of a six-year-old girl? Maybe that's why Katie and I clicked so well.

He lifted a shoulder. "You need to fix it."

"Sorry if I'm not sure how to fix an invisible color shroud that only you can see." I scoffed, finishing my breakfast and dropping some cash on the table. "Are we done here?"

"Guess so," he said.

And I left him sitting there, my head in an even darker place than it had been when we'd sat down, full of questions about glittery auras and the game.

If I didn't even have hockey now, what the fuck was left?

That night I lay on my back staring at the ceiling after a long, punishing workout at the gym in my building. I'd exhausted myself, but my brain wouldn't quit.

I wondered how Clara's new job was going.

I wondered if she hated me.

I wondered about Katie. What had Clara told her about me leaving so suddenly? Was she sad? Did she miss me at all?

And Mom. She'd looked like she was going to cry when I'd told them I was going. Dad had sat in his chair looking mildly annoyed with me, but it was Mom I worried about. Now that I knew Dad wasn't doing well, I understood how much of a load she was carrying. And even though it hurt that she hadn't trusted me to be there when she'd needed me the first time, this time I was consciously walking away.

I made a mental note to call her, to check in. Maybe I could help somehow without physically being there. Maybe Dad could use a nurse or something? Some kind of trainer to strengthen his heart?

I pushed out a deep breath, understanding how difficult it would be for Mom to convince him to do anything good for himself. He was stubborn and angry, and possibly depressed. I'd tried to strike up a variety of conversations while we'd worked on the fence, but he was like a stone wall. It was hard to watch, and it was like he'd decided he wasn't worth the effort it would require to change any of that. I hated seeing him like that.

When sleep didn't feel like it was anywhere in the same four state radius as I was, I rolled over and snatched my phone off the bedside table, dialing.

"Hello?"

"Doc."

"Hello, Sylvester. It's pretty late. Is everything okay?"

I glanced at the clock. It was after ten. "I'm sorry. I can call back in the morning."

"You have me now. How are things going?"

"Um. Yeah. Not good."

"You went home for the summer, didn't you? Are you still at your childhood home?"

"No. Too much commuting. I moved back to my condo. Needed to focus."

"I see. How is that going?" Her voice was almost as monotone as Mizzoni's, and I wondered if it was some kind of strategy to get you to talk. Maybe they were trying to get me to tell them things that might shock them, that might earn me a variation in vocal octave.

"Yeah. Good."

"So you're calling me at ten o'clock at night to reassure me that things are going well. Are you trying to reassure yourself, maybe?"

"Things are good."

"Hockey players generally don't reach out to me when things are actually good."

"Right. Well." I took a breath told her the bare bones of my summer. Clara. Katie. Being home.

"That's a lot. Let's start at the beginning. Tell me what happened with the woman next door. Your high school crush."

Clara's face moved to the center of my mind. It always hovered nearby, on the far reaches of my consciousness where I did my best to keep it. But now it was here, and my heart cramped a bit as I thought about her. About Katie.

"Nothing happened really. We spent a little time together. And that was it."

"Did you develop a relationship with her, Sylvester?"

"We're neighbors. That is a relationship."

The doctor said nothing, and I heard in the silence that she wasn't interested in my bullshit.

"Yes. We . . . dated, I guess. For a while."

"And has that concluded?"

"Yeah. It has."

"Who ended it?"

"I did."

"Tell me why."

I squeezed my eyes shut. "It was affecting my game. You saw the exhibition match. I blew it. This was supposed to be the last year on my contract, and I might not be ready to retire after all. I need to stay in the game." Since the idea of the MBA was out at this point.

"Your behavior was her fault? Clara's?"

"I was distracted."

"I see."

"I thought she wasn't there, and I was looking around for her when I should have been focusing. My mind was a mess."

"I understand. And what happened before that game?"

"What do you mean? We warmed up. Like usual."

"Outside of hockey, Sylvester. Things were going well at home? With your family? With Clara?"

"No," I admitted, realizing I was about to tell her everything.

"Things were shit." And then I did it. I opened the floodgates and talked. I told her about Dad. About my family not believing I could handle the news and still play hockey. I told her about the fucking MBA, about the project I'd tanked until Clara had helped me with it. And then about seeing Jason, and having to give up the whole program now that I was outed.

I talked so long I wasn't sure if she was even still on the line, but once the words started, they wouldn't stop coming.

"So I came back here, and I'm just focusing on the game and nothing else. It's the only thing I have. The only thing I've ever been good at."

"I get it," Hasselbeck said. "So you actually had quite a lot on your mind at the exhibition game. And I do understand how that could be distracting and affect your play."

"Right. It did."

"And so now that you're back where you started, now that you've excised the distractions from your day to day, your game has improved, right? Practices are going well? You're back where you were?"

"I get the feeling you already know the answer." Frustration had me pacing the apartment.

"Sylvester, there's a very real chance that running away from the things that are difficult doesn't eliminate them. Think of them like actual physical obstacles. You can turn back to avoid them, but then you don't make any real progress on your path, right?"

I felt my eyebrows pulling together. I did not like where she was going.

"They're still there. And until you actually deal with the obstacles, they'll be in your way, making it impossible to get any real clarity to focus on anything."

"Deal with them."

"Talk to your family. Talk to Clara."

I sighed. I knew she was right, but talking to them could reveal the things they really believed about me—the things I was pretty sure I already knew. "I'm talking to you. You're supposed to help with this stuff."

"No, Sylvester. My job is to help identify things that might interfere with your game. And we've done that. Your job is to handle them."

"Great."

"They love you, Sylvester. Your family certainly does, and I suspect Clara might too. What if talking to them all results in a really marvelous outcome? What if you end up getting everything you want? What if you end up happy?"

I thought about that, but I couldn't see it. All I could see was how much I'd already disappointed them all by not being anything more than exactly what I was — a hockey player.

"Thanks, Doc. I'll think about it."

"Good night, Sylvester."

I slid the phone back on the nightstand and switched off the light, not bothering to get up to brush my teeth. At least now I was mentally exhausted enough to sleep.

CHAPTER 23

CLARA

LAWYERS HAVE POWERFUL MAGIC

I knew the first time Sly touched me that I was going to be broken.

Because I never expected that he would stay. I'm not a fairy tale girl, and the writing had been on the wall for us since high school.

He's the jock, the object of every woman's desire.

I'm the nerd, the girl no one really notices until they need help with math.

It didn't matter that a decade had passed. Or that I had a daughter of my own.

And it didn't matter that Sly had said all the things I'd always dreamed of hearing him say. Except one.

In the end, it was a fling. And I had to be okay with that.

Only I wasn't okay at all.

I found myself staring into space at my desk, losing track of myself and my work constantly. And at home, I was short with Katie, which she didn't deserve.

Because if we were honest? She'd lost him too.

"Do you think Silllvesssterrr will be at Miss Violet's house today?" Katie faced every new day with optimism about Sly's return. That was where her heartbreak over losing him differed from mine. I knew it was over.

"No, honey. He had to go back to his real home, remember? To get back to his real life."

"Playing hockey." She frowned when she stated this.

"Yep. To play hockey."

"I hate hockey."

I wished it was as easy for me to take my anger and hurt at Sly's departure and aim it somewhere else. At hockey or at summer or skating. But I was too old to transfer my feelings so easily. I was mad at him.

I'd picked up my phone hundreds of times in the weeks since he'd gone, planning to text him or call, to tell him exactly what I thought of him slinking away without a goodbye, leaving me here alone. But I'd always been stopped by the futility of it.

I knew, didn't I? I knew when he came that it would be temporary. He was famous. And he didn't live here. And there was nothing in our past—beyond his recent words to the contrary—to suggest that anything had changed in the way he saw me. Or the way he saw women in general.

All that said, I didn't regret it. Even the empty ache inside me didn't remove the glee and validation that had come from being the center of his attention, even if it was only for a little bit. I knew it was pathetic, but I couldn't help it. I would always have that knowledge. For a little while, the man I'd loved my whole life had chosen me.

Zara and Beck were staying next door the weekend before the wedding, and Zara had suggested that we use Saturday to head to the boutiques downtown to find Katie the perfect flower girl dress.

"You ready?" Zara asked, bouncing on my front steps at exactly ten Saturday morning. She looked gorgeous and happy, her pale skin lit as if from within by a luminescence that I was sure came from her heart. I tried to be happy for her—and I was. It just hurt a bit to smile.

"Yes!" Katie pushed past me to join Zara on the steps. "I hope we find something sparkly! With a lot of pockets!"

Zara and I exchanged an amused glance as I stepped out and locked the door behind me.

"You never know," Zara said. "The bridesmaids are all wearing shades of grey and silver," she told us. "And the accent colors are peach and dark green."

"That sounds gorgeous," I said.

"I like green," Katie told us as we climbed into my car. Zara had offered to drive, but Violet had Katie's booster in her car, and it seemed like a lot of trouble to move it again. I was happy that Sly had remembered to pull it from his car before he disappeared, though a tiny part of me liked the thought of him turning around to back out and seeing it there. A subtle reminder of the two girls he'd spent time with back home in Half Full.

"How are you doing?" Zara asked in a low voice as we drove toward Main Street.

"Oh, you know. Good. Work is a little slow now that I'm in the office all the time." I did my best not to sound grumpy.

"I meant with everything else, really. I know Sly kind of snuck away. Beck told me." Zara's voice held a soft note of sympathy and I wanted to push it back at her, tell her I didn't want it.

Except talking with her was different than the discussions I'd had with Andie and Betty, who were furious on my behalf. She was on the inside.

"It's fine, really. I knew we were just a temporary thing while he was home."

She was looking at the side of my face and I could feel her frown. "Why, though? Did something happen?"

"What, to make him leave?"

"Silllvessssterrr had to go back to play hockey," Katie told her. I wished I believed that was the only reason.

"We didn't have a fight or anything," I told Zara in a low voice, doing my best to keep Katie out of my misery. "But it was like something shifted in him when he found out about Sam being sick."

"Huh." Zara sounded as confused as I felt by this information. "Well, you're still going to come to the wedding, right?"

"I'm IN the wedding," Katie reminded her.

"I know you'll be there," Zara laughed, turning around to smile at my daughter. "I'm hoping your mom will come too."

"It feels a bit like an intrusion now, to be honest." I'd thought a lot about it. Sly hadn't said anything about having asked me to be his date. I assume that was off. "I'll just pick Katie up after the ceremony, I think."

"I won't hear of it," Zara said. "And I know Violet will pitch a fit. No. You have to come."

I pulled up in front of the little stretch of dress shops along Half Full's Main Street downtown. If we couldn't find a dress for Katie here, Boomsmack had a couple of high end kids' shops I thought might work. I'd put off the dress shopping too long, and now I felt bad that Zara had to get involved, but she made it seem like a fun girls' day, as if she had nothing else to do.

"Look at that!" Katie cooed at the window display, where there actually was a little girl's dress that might work.

"Let's go try it on!" Zara suggested.

We got lucky. The dress was perfect, and I was relieved not to have to take up any more of Zara's time. "One stop," I said. "That was easy."

"We're not done," Zara said. "You need a dress too."

I shook my head. "It doesn't feel right," I told her. "It will be awkward."

She frowned at me and let out a soft sigh. "What if I told you that I have inside information? That I know for a fact Sly is a mess after leaving you, and that I really don't think it's over. And neither does Beck or Violet."

I refused to let her words wind their way into my too-hopeful heart. "He hasn't even texted. Not once. He didn't say goodbye."

"I'm not telling you that he's become super emotionally intelligent since you last saw him," Zara said with a wry smile. "But I guess I'm asking you a question. If there was a chance, would you want it?"

My stupid heart pounded against my chest as if trying to answer her question, worried that I would lie and it would lose its chance. I dropped her gaze, glanced at Katie poking around the shoe rack on one side of the store, and finally said, "yes."

But then I thought about it.

"But even if there was another chance, what's to stop him from doing the same thing again if something upsets him? I can't make things work with someone whose first instinct is to run away."

Zara tilted her head to one side. "That's fair," she said. "But maybe he needs a chance to hear your side. So he can explain his."

I sighed, the thought of there being sides at all just feeling suddenly exhausting and depressing. Before I could sink too deeply into my funk, Zara took my arm and pulled me to where Katie was admiring a six-inch platform shoe that looked like part of a costume.

"Your mom needs a pretty dress for the wedding too," Zara told my daughter. "Let's find one for her, okay?"

Katie clapped and took Zara's outstretched hand. And then I allowed them to drag me through every boutique in Half Full and half of those in Boomsmack to find just the right dress to wear so that Sly could ignore me at his brother's wedding.

As we pulled back into the driveway in front of my house, I looked over at Zara, who was still glowing. "Thanks for coming with us," I told her. "It was fun." It would have been fun, anyway, if Sly hadn't overshadowed the whole event.

"I'm just glad I talked you into coming," she said. "Beck and Violet will be so happy." She inclined her head. "And I bet Sly will be too."

I sighed. I wasn't going to get my hopes up. What in the world was I going to hope for, anyway? That he'd move in with his parents permanently? Give up hockey? Become the father Katie didn't have? It was all a little ridiculous. Better to let a fling be a fling, even if my heart hadn't gotten the memo.

That week at work, I came to a realization.

I was miserable.

It started when Betty called in to report that one of the cubs we'd thought had been successfully placed had been found alone two days in a row. She tracked him all week and confirmed that he wasn't with the mama we'd placed him with or his new siblings. He'd been abandoned.

It happened sometimes, and it broke my heart every single time. He was too old now to try to place again, which left us with a couple options. Most bears were equipped to survive on their own after about six months of age. This little guy was right on that border, so we could just leave him, hoping he built a den in fall and avoided danger until then. If he survived winter, he'd most likely be fine. The other option was to bring him in and potentially offer him to a zoo, but that was an all-else-fails option.

Betty came back into the office every day, reporting what she'd found and delivering the data she'd collected. And every day, I wished to be the one doing the tracking, the one seeing that little cub with my own eyes and determining his future. Betty was more than competent, and so was her new partner, Hal. But they were doing what I loved. And it was hard to accept.

I couldn't sit behind a desk all day. I couldn't file reports and edit typos and be the supervisor for those doing the work I really wanted to do.

"You're sure about this, Clara?" Paul asked when I told him.

"Yes."

"It's a pay cut," he reminded me.

"I know. I'll figure it out. I just want to be back in the field. It's what I really love."

He nodded, sighing. "It'll be a little while, then," he said. "Until I figure out who can replace you in the office."

"Thanks, Paul." Knowing I'd be back in the field made me happy, and so I headed back to my desk with a renewed sense of hope. It would make things tougher with Katie. But if her mother was miserable all the time, that would make things harder for her too, right?

The wedding approached, despite my best efforts to ignore it. On one hand, I couldn't wait to see Katie tossing flower petals and skipping down the aisle in her official role as flower girl. But on the other, I already knew how handsome Sly would look in his suit, and I could anticipate how horribly awkward it would be to see him again.

I contemplated numerous ways to get out of going, but having Katie in the wedding made it a little complicated. I was her ride, not to mention her guardian. I didn't really have a choice. Plus, I'd pretty much promised Zara that I would attend.

And so, on Saturday morning, I packed our bags, and we headed to the little lakefront resort where Zara and Beck were getting married. It was three hours from Half Full, which meant spending the night. Zara had been kind enough to reserve one of the little cabins by the lake, holding it for me even when I'd assured her two weeks ago that I wouldn't need it. She was right, though. It would be a long drive to make twice in one day. I'd stay the night and we'd leave early in the morning.

Now, as we drove between the adorable cabins, taking in the

pristine greenery of the setting and seeing the water sparkle just off the little decks of the A-frame structures, I was glad. It would be a fun adventure for us both. I would just do my best to avoid Sly.

No problem.

We checked in during the late morning, and the resort was quiet. Katie and I explored the lakefront and then, at about noon, went inside our cabin to get ready for the ceremony.

All the events were taking place on the resort property, and as I helped Katie into her new fancy dress shoes, I could hear activity ramping up outside as more guests began to arrive and preparations got underway in the big reception space around the lake a ways from our cabin.

I showered and curled my hair, taking a little extra time with my appearance, as if it would make any difference at all. I knew Sly would not see me in a little extra eye shadow and change his mind about everything in his life and where I might fit in it, but it felt a bit like strengthening my armor. I'd look amazing enough to survive whatever the day might throw at me.

I was here for Zara and Beck. And Katie. And I would do my best to be happy for them and to enjoy myself.

"You ready?" I asked Katie as I slipped on my own heels.

She didn't answer. She was staring up at me with big blue eyes shining. "Mama, you look beautiful. Like a movie star or a lawyer." Katie had recently been considering a career in law because someone had told her that women lawyers were very powerful. She considered this a high compliment, I knew, though I also suspected that she thought lawyers might have magic similar to wizards, thanks to the use of the word "powerful."

"Thanks, bear. You look very beautiful, too. Like a tiny lawyer."

She beamed and then pulled me to the full-length mirror on the back of the bathroom door and we stood there, admiring ourselves and each other for a long moment.

"I can't wait to see Sylvester," she told me as we finally moved toward the door of the cabin.

My heart ached inside me. How did I prepare her for the fact that he might not react to her quite the same way he had before? I didn't know, so I didn't try.

"I know, honey." I locked the cabin and tucked the key into my little purse, and we stepped down off the porch, joining the scattered flow of guests heading for the chapel at one end of the resort. Zara had told me to drop Katie with her and Violet in the bride's room inside the front doors.

I knocked, and Violet answered, beaming at me and Katie, and grasping her hands in front of her at her chest. "Oh don't you look beautiful?" she asked us both. "We'll take good care of this little princess—"

"Lawyer," Katie corrected.

"Um, yes. You go and enjoy yourself, Clara, and we'll see you after the ceremony."

Once I'd delivered Katie, I turned back to the main entrance of the intimate little space, steeling myself with a deep breath.

The chapel was a big A-frame structure, like many of the resort buildings, only the walls were inlaid with stained glass showing forest scenes and giving the rows of benches inside an ethereal glow. Guests were filing in as a string quartet at the front of the space played classical music, and a deep calm filled me as I breathed it all in.

Sam greeted me at the end of one row, taking my hands in his. He looked healthier than I'd seen him, a nice flush in his cheeks.

"I'm so glad to see you. You look beautiful," he said. It was the most words I thought Sly's dad had ever spoken to me.

"You look well," I told him. "Thanks so much for having me. I'm so happy for Beck."

He nodded. "Good to see one of my sons doing it right."

He released my hands, gesturing for me to sit, and moved on to greet other guests as I turned his words over in my head. I'd always thought he was the reason Sly was so singularly focused on hockey. That it was the thing his dad cared about most—sports. Did we both have it wrong?

I sat, focusing on the little program in my hands, and looking up now and then to smile at those joining me in the pews surrounding where I sat.

After a bit, the music stopped and shifted, and I looked up toward the altar.

Sly stood there, his dark gaze trained on me, and a full-body shiver passed through me.

He looked so handsome. And, I realized as my gaze met his, he looked determined.

CHAPTER 24
SLY

BEAR WRESTLING AND WEDDINGS:
THE PERFECT COMBO

She came.

Thanks to Zara and Beck, and my mom, she came. I knew Clara didn't decide to attend my brother's wedding to see me. In fact, Zara had reported back that seeing me was the number one reason why she probably wouldn't attend.

But she came.

And seeing her there, the light from the stained glass reflecting down on her pale hair and glowing skin, made my heart stop a couple times as I stood at the front of the little chapel.

I'd wanted to call her. Of course I had.

I'd picked up the phone to text a thousand times. But how do you explain how wrong you were about everything on the phone? How do you apologize if you can't see her eyes, if you can't be sure that she really understands?

I could have gone to her, of course. But with hockey, and the efforts it took to get my MBA program back on track, I needed the time. I wanted everything to be set up before I made promises I couldn't keep.

It had to wait. But now, she was here, and as far as I knew, everything was ready.

The string quartet was playing, but they'd shifted from classical to classical-sounding covers of popular songs. Zara's parents walked down the aisle, their smiles wide and relaxed, as the strings played—of all things—Macklemore's "Can't Hold Us."

Zara and Beck had decided exactly how things would go on their big day, and aside from the non-traditional music, they'd also planned the whole aisle-walking thing to be a bit different. Beck insisted that he wanted to walk down the aisle, saying it was silly that it was only women who usually got the experience. I pointed out that groomsmen usually did too, and I guess somehow that earned me a stationary spot up front with the other guys.

Whatever. Beck and Zara could do their wedding just the way they wanted. Mine would be my way. Or actually, I didn't care at all. As long as the woman walking down the aisle to me was a certain blue-eyed blonde who'd I'd loved since I was seventeen years old.

The bridesmaids were next, Zara's sorority and work friends, I assumed. I hadn't met most of them, since my brother and his fiancée hadn't felt a rehearsal was required, and I'd been mostly absent these last few weeks while I got my shit straightened out.

The music shifted, switching to what I was pretty sure was "Earned It" by the Wknd, and there was Katie. I could feel my face stretch into a huge smile upon seeing her there, her hair curled and pulled partly up around her face, wearing a sparkly green dress, and holding a basket of flower petals. She flung them to each side as she walked, taking a moment to turn and make sure she was scattering some down the path behind her. She was focused and meticulous, taking her job so seriously—until she spotted me.

And then my heart nearly fell out of my chest when she made a funny little shriek, dumped out the rest of the petals, and practically sprinted to where I stood, flinging herself into my body so hard I had no choice but to catch her.

"Sylvesterrrrrrrr," she wailed against my neck as I hugged her.

Good thing my brother and Zara didn't worry about everything being just right because I was pretty sure this part wasn't scripted.

"Hey Katie," I whispered to her. Her little arms were locked around my neck and she was squeezing so tightly I was a little worried she might successfully cut off my air flow.

"You left," she said, in a voice so sad and dejected that any part of me that had been certain I'd done the right thing bowed his head and left.

"I know. I'm sorry."

"I missed you so much."

"I missed you too."

The quartet seemed to be waiting for this little interlude to end so that Zara could make her way down the aisle.

"Hey," I said softly. "If I put you down so Zara can go ahead and finish up her wedding, I promise we'll hang out later at the party, okay?"

Katie relaxed her grip a little, perhaps remembering that there was a reason we were all gathered here today and choking me out was not it. "Okay."

I slipped her down to the ground, and she gathered her dropped basket from the ground, throwing a few more petals left in the bottom, and then took her seat next to Zara's parents.

I straightened my tie, my eyes finding Clara's in the crowd.

She didn't look happy, and it made me want to interrupt everything again and go to her right then. Her deep blue eyes shone, and I wondered if I'd made her cry. Had she cried over me these last weeks?

The crowd got to their feet and I lost my view of Clara as the quartet shifted to a song I couldn't quite identify. Beck stepped to the center of the aisle, ready to receive his bride, and Zara appeared at the end of the little chapel.

She wore a simple, straight sheath dress, and her dark hair was topped with a wide, airy veil that made her look just like an angel. Or a model. She wore a wide, self-assured smile, and as she moved slowly down the aisle, she had eyes only for my brother. I was so happy for him, and just a tiny bit jealous. I wanted this. All of this.

As the quartet shifted, I realized they were playing an old Tom Petty song, "Here Comes my Girl," which they drew to a close just as Zara reached Beck and they both turned to face the officiant.

There was no giving away of the bride or promising to obey—which I was glad about. So much of the tradition wrapped up in weddings seemed to be about women giving up their independence, and I knew that wasn't what would happen between Zara and Beckett. And it wasn't what I wanted, either.

If Clara wanted to wrestle a couple bears just before we got married, I'd be totally fine with it. I didn't want to change her, I had realized. I loved her because of exactly who she was.

I also realized I was way ahead of myself. The woman I was planning the bear-wrestling wedding with wasn't currently speaking to me, so there were a few details still to work out.

Zara and Beckett said their vows and kissed, and the chapel exploded into cheers and applause, and suddenly, Katie was back at my side. She was the only thing I hadn't really planned into what was going to come next, since I hadn't been able to coordinate with her ahead of time. Now though, I leaned down and whispered into her ear, explaining what was about to happen and asking if she'd be willing to help me.

"Yes, yes, yes, yes!"

Katie was excited about my plan. I gave her a high five, slipped something from my pocket into her hand, and sent her back to her mom.

The crowd had begun filing out of the chapel, and Zara and Beck were getting a few pictures taken up front, so I stood nearby sweating and trying to force myself to take deep, calming breaths as Dr. Hasselbeck always suggested.

CHAPTER 25

CLARA

WOMBAT ACAPELLA

Zara and Beck's ceremony had been wonderful, and so perfectly them. I loved everything from the music to the way they rearranged all the things so many people took for granted because there was a way that better suited their desire, their unique love.

My own wedding had been traditional. Every single part had been scripted, and it had felt as if I was just an actress in a complex production that Zach's mother was orchestrating. My own parents had gone along with it, assuming it was what I wanted. And that had been the problem. I didn't know what I wanted back then. I just wanted to be the girl someone chose, I guessed. And so I did what I thought was expected.

But I was done doing what was expected.

And so, as I filed out of the little chapel, accepting a glass of champagne from the waiter standing on the top of the steps, I decided that I'd find the bride and groom, wish them well, and then talk Katie into skipping the reception. We didn't have to go. Her part was over. So now, I might like to just enjoy the beautiful setting for one night, and then go back home.

I told myself it had nothing to do with seeing Sly, or with the painful realizations that seeing him had pushed me even further toward. That I loved him, for one. Really loved him. Before, it had been a teenaged crush on the guy I thought he was, on the guy so many of my high school peers professed to be in love with. But now? I knew him. I'd seen past the facade. And I loved him.

But it didn't matter.

"Mommy." Katie was holding something, thrusting it upward toward me.

"What's this, bear?" I took the little scrap of paper and held it, smiling down at the beautiful little girl before me. "You did so good, honey. Did you have fun?"

"Mommy." Katie's voice was stern. "The paper."

I shook my head, making a face at her. "Okay." Uncrumpling the little scrap of paper and reading it.

Go to the big tree at the edge of the lake between the chapel and the next cabin over.

I looked around, confused. "What?"

Katie had a funny look on her face.

"What is this?" I asked her.

She shrugged. "I didn't read it. I was just supposed to give it to you."

"Said who?" I asked her.

The little rascal just shrugged again.

Zara and Beckett had emerged from the chapel, and I took a moment to hug them each, ignoring the confusing little note in my hand and doing my best not to feel a burning gaze on my back. Sly stood just to one side of the steps, watching us.

I waved at him, not trusting myself to actually talk to him without breaking down. I wasn't going to waste any more tears on Sly Remington, though. So I took a deep breath and moved away.

"Mom!" Katie's little voice was insistent now, and she was tugging my free hand. "What does it say?"

I showed it to her.

"So let's go." She pulled me toward the lake. I let her, afraid to take too many mental guesses about what this was. I'd seen too many romantic movies for sure, and the last thing I needed was to let my heart carry me away. But what else could this be?

Sly's face had given nothing away. In fact, when I'd glanced his way, he'd looked almost angry. So this note . . . could it be from him?

We followed the path toward the edge of the lake, and found two chairs set up on a deck just at the water's edge. They faced back toward the resort, and as we approached, Katie dropped my hand and scooped fresh petals out of the basket that still dangled from her arm.

"Wait," she commanded, and then she sprinkled them between me and the biggest chair on the shore.

"Katie, what is this?"

She shook her little head and took the smaller chair. "Sit down."

I headed toward her, my heart accelerating inside me uncomfortably. And just as I sat, Stephano Mizzoni stepped out from behind a tree, nearly giving me a heart attack. I was about to speak, but he opened his mouth, and the most beautiful voice I'd ever heard emerged.

He was singing?

The lyrics to "A Thousand Years" were familiar to me—it was one of the most romantic songs I knew. About someone who'd known they loved someone else as long as they'd lived. About how they'd loved them for a thousand years, and would go on loving for a thousand more.

But hearing Stephano sing the first few lines, a serious look on his face as I sat here on the side of a lake? It was surreal.

And then another of Sly's teammates—Deck Gillespie, maybe? Carried a little table out from behind the cabin closest to us and set it before me, placing a puck on the table top.

I was about to ask what it was all about when his mouth opened and he sang the next verse. Katie cackled aloud in her excitement as Stephano's voice joined Deck's, and he stepped closer and deposited a second puck on top of the first one.

What the hell was going on?

Other men were emerging from between the trees now, and the wedding crowd started to follow the sounds of singing. I realized the guys had lapel mics and the string quartet had actually picked up the melody and moved close by on one side.

Tears were pressing against the backs of my eyes, but I still wasn't sure why this was happening. And where was Sly? His whole team was here, stacking pucks on this little table in front of me and singing . . . Who knew the Wilcox Wombats could sing like this?

INTERLUDE

JULIUS

It was common knowledge the Wombats had won the All-League Acapella competition a few years in a row now, though the entire competition had been recently abandoned due to lack of interest.

It seemed hockey fans were not necessarily the same folks who'd sent my favorite movie, *Pitch Perfect*, to fame.

Still, the competition had been fierce (more fights broke out than in the movies, that was for sure). And the Wombats had been on top.

CHAPTER 26

CLARA

STACKING POOP SAYS I'M SORRY

And then he appeared and my heart tried to escape my chest, pounding to get near him again. He was walking down the path I'd followed, a puck in one hand and a red rose in the other. And he was singing!

I'd never heard Sly sing before, though he'd mentioned that the team sometimes sang karaoke after practices.

His voice was low and clear, and it pulled at something inside me. Maybe it was the words—about moving a step closer, about time bringing one heart to another . . . Maybe it was the way his dark eyes found mine and held them as he sang these words to me.

I felt the tears escape, and Katie leaned toward me. "It's okay, Mommy. It's just Sylvesterrrr."

I nodded, a nervous laugh escaping me.

The whole wedding crowd was around us now, Zara and Beck, Violet and Sam all grinning widely as Sly got to the end of the song, and every single voice joined his for the final chorus, raising a gorgeous kind of noise up through the trees along the lakeside, and ending in fading strains of violin when they were done.

Sly was standing right in front of me now, and he put the puck he held on the top of what had become a very tall and somewhat precarious tower.

"Clara," he said, in a voice so low I wasn't sure the gathered crowd could hear. "I knew just saying I was sorry wasn't enough. I knew that in order to apologize to you, to tell you how much you really mean to me . . ." he paused, squeezed his eyes shut for a moment, and took a deep breath as if gathering his strength. "I knew that to tell you that I love you, that I think I've always loved you, I needed a gesture."

I barely heard the last part as the word love carved itself through my chest, finding my heart and landing there, making a permanent mark.

"I . . ." I shook my head, finding his eyes and never wanting to drop his gaze. "I don't . . . I can't . . ." The teenaged girl inside me was keeping me from forming any actual words.

I loved Sly Remington with an impossible abundance. I'd known it since I was a girl, and it had only deepened over time. First, he'd been a hero to my teenaged idealist. Then, he'd been an unknown icon, a wistful juxtaposition to the life I'd chosen by mistake, an easy place to look to consider what I might have had instead. And now? He was before me telling me he loved me.

I stood slowly, unsure if my legs could still work in this alternate universe I was in now. "I'm having a hard time making words work," I told him quietly.

A hopeful smile lifted one side of his mouth. "Maybe you could just nod? I'm kind of dying here . . . Do you think you might maybe dance with me? At the reception?"

I nodded.

A little ripple of tangible relief moved through the crowd as the same relief washed across Sly's face.

"Am I pushing my luck if I ask if maybe I could hold you for just a second right now?"

I shook my head.

Sly stepped closer and slipped his arms around me. I couldn't speak, but my body hadn't forgotten what to do. I moved into him, relief flooding me as if my entire being had been waiting for exactly this kind of rescue.

The crowd around us broke into hoots and applause, and I popped one eye open around Sly's shoulder to see them starting to wander away, back to the reception. I was relieved—this was not what they'd come for and they needed to go back to celebrating Zara and Beck.

Sly's teammates remained though, and after a second, I cleared my throat and we stepped apart.

"Are you going to kiss him, Mommy?" Katie was bouncing on her toes at our side.

I smiled at her, and then tilted my chin up. "I think I should," I told her, looking into Sly's handsome face. "That okay with you?"

He nodded.

The kiss was quick, but it cemented something between us, and my heart felt like it was slowly mending, like all the hopeful broken parts were finding their way back together.

"I love you, Clara," Sly whispered in my ear.

I nodded again, but I knew that wasn't enough now. "I love you too," I told him quietly. "I think I always have."

Katie clapped and bounced some more. "Will I get to be a flower girl again?" she asked. I tried not to let myself picture it, still unsure of this thing between us, of what it meant for our future. But the idea of the three of us forming a real family? It was all I wanted.

The team had stepped closer now, and I broke out of Sly's embrace, feeling a little silly standing next to the tower of pucks with all these burly men around watching me kiss their teammate. "Hi guys," I said.

"Clara," Freddy Elks replied. "Welcome to the Wombats."

"Clara," Stephano said, nodding his head at me.

The whole team actually welcomed me, and it felt like an official ceremony of sorts. "Does this mean I'm allowed at your parties now?"

"Of course," Stephano said. "Officially."

"Can I ask a question?"

"Sure," Sly said, looking happier and more relaxed than I thought I'd ever seen him.

"What's with the tower of pucks?"

"It's symbolic," Tyler Cornwall explained.

"Because we're wombats," Chris Houstein went on.

I shook my head. They couldn't mean . . .

"You're a biologist, right?" Cade Simpson asked, his wide grin apparent, even beneath the enormous beard.

"I am," I confirmed.

"Then you know how wombats communicate, and how they court a potential mate, right?" He nodded slowly.

"By . . . stacking their cube-shaped feces," I replied, staring at the tower.

The team all cheered.

"The tower is supposed to be your poop?" Katie asked Sly.

I couldn't suppress the laugh that escaped me at Sly's indignant face. "No." He shook his head and rubbed the back of his neck, looking around. "I mean, kind of?"

I laughed harder.

"Guys," he said, sounding a tiny bit angry now. "We might need to rethink this whole symbolic act thing . . ."

I pulled him close to me and kissed him again. "I love it," I told him. "And I love you."

"Can we go to the party now?" Katie asked.

"Yeah," I said, glancing at Sly. "I guess we'd better."

"Thanks, guys," Sly told his teammates.

"Any time," Cade replied, reaching to shake Sly's hand and then giving me a kiss on the cheek.

We said goodbye to the team, and then Katie and Sly and I headed for the reception, the three of us walking hand in hand as a towering table of puck-poop sat in the dying light near the lakeside.

My brother's wedding was pretty fucking awesome. Probably because my brother was awesome, and he'd found a woman who perfectly complimented him. I was biased in many ways, of course, not the least of which was because Beck and Zara had been kind enough to allow me to momentarily hijack their wedding for my own selfish purposes.

"It wasn't selfish," Zara said later as we finally sat down to have some dinner at their reception. "You were a total beast while you and Clara were apart, and we wanted to have a fun wedding. We had no choice but to help."

I dropped my jaw open and stared at her like this was shocking news, but I knew she was right. I'd been miserable.

"I have to thank you too," Clara said. "For everything." She and Katie sat on each side of me and for the first time in weeks, it felt like things were level and right.

Beck and Zara shared a smile and clasped hands between the chairs where they sat side-by-side across from us. The reception was informal, a buffet and open seating, so there was no head table or official duties to be done now that they were hitched.

"If I can help my stubborn superstar big brother find even a tiny fraction of the happiness I've found, I'll feel like I've done something good," Beck said.

"You do lots of good," Zara told him, leaning in to kiss his cheek.

They shared an intimate look then that made my heart flop around inside my chest, and I reached for Clara without planning to, my whole being driving me to touch her. More than ever, I wanted to find a place we could be alone, to reassure myself that this was real, that she was mine.

Wedding receptions—even the most unconventional—follow a certain rhythm, and as much as I wanted to hoist Clara over my shoulder and run away with her, I couldn't. Not yet. Plus, I was doing my best to temper my expectations around any alone time, given that Katie was here with us too.

Despite the casual seating and non-scripted events of the evening, I felt like part of my obligation as best man and brother was to give a proper toast, so once everyone was seated, I signaled the DJ. He brought me the microphone, and I stood, moving to the center of the room where I could see everyone.

"Hey there," I began, feeling a little bit awkward now that all eyes were on me. Normally when people were watching me I was wearing skates and pads. I felt naked and vulnerable, as silly as that was. "I'm Sylvester, Beckett's older, wiser, and much more handsome brother."

That earned a little chuckle that relaxed me a bit, and I glanced to Clara to find her bright happy gaze on me, banishing any remaining nerves.

"In reality," I continued, "Beckett's had me beat my whole life with the single exception of that one time when I was actually born first. Since the day he arrived, he's been kinder, smarter . . . hell, maybe even funnier than I could ever manage to be.

"I remember one time, when we were pretty small, the family went to some lake for a picnic. Hell, maybe it was here—Beckett was better at geography too, I guess."

Another little laugh rippled through the crowd and I met my brother's eyes. He shook his head just a little, disagreeing with me. Or potentially dreading the story I was about to tell.

"Well, I'd told the little guy, who maybe was about four at the time, that it was pretty likely that we'd bump into a Bigfoot, being out in the wilderness like this. Needless to say, he was terrified, which I found pretty amusing at the ripe old age of six. I wracked my brain to see how I could amuse myself even more, and told Beck that the only way to guarantee that Bigfoot wouldn't haul you away and eat you was to be naked when he found you."

I switched hands with the microphone and turned to face some of the other tables, getting into the story now. "So Beck stripped down as we were eating Mom's ham sandwiches and refused to put his clothes back on, no matter what either of my parents did. I took my shirt off in solidarity.

"But here's how Beck won this one too. After lunch, we were exploring around the lakeside, Mom and Dad sitting right nearby, watching us, having given up on getting their youngest into any clothes at all. And one of us must've stepped on an old rotten log or something where a bunch of wasps were nesting."

A worried little gasp went up from the crowd.

"You'd think I'd be better off, partially covered like I was. But you'd be wrong. Beck started screaming and running around, getting Dad's attention, and pretty soon I was screaming and dancing too, because the wasps were everywhere. Dad grabbed Beck and me and ran to the water, taking us both in with him, which sent most of the wasps headed in the other direction since I guess they're not great swimmers.

"Anyway, once we're in the water and the wasps were gone, Beck was crying over the welts he'd gotten all over his chest and legs. But me? I was still screaming and flailing around, which made my dad pretty pissed."

I grinned at Dad, who shook his head at me. He was grinning back, though, and something loosened in my chest. I hadn't seen Dad smile in a while.

"You see, I still had on shorts and underwear. And the wasps had gotten inside those as I'd stood basically on top of their nest, and when Dad had pulled us into the water, they were still there. So then not only were those things pissed that I'd stepped on their nest, they were furious because I was slowly drowning them in my pants."

Most of the guests were laughing now, despite their pained expressions.

"So you see . . . Beck won that one too. I ended up with wasp stings in places we just don't talk about in polite company."

I bowed my head for a quick second in silent reverence for my nuts, which had, luckily, recovered from the incident.

"And what we're here to celebrate today? It's just one more example of my brother winning. Because Zara? She's everything. Sweet, funny, kind, smart—and last I heard, she beat him at just about every game they played. Which tells me that he's found his match."

I raised a glass of champagne in their direction.

"Please join me in welcoming Zara to the Remington family, and in wishing both Zara and Beck many wins in their future together."

There was clapping and cheering, and I handed the mic back to the DJ. He started some music, and just as I was about to return to my table and see if I could convince Clara to dance with me so I could feel her up as best I could in front of a crowd of people, Dad signaled me from where he and Mom were sitting.

I glanced over at Clara and pointed to my parents. She nodded and raised her glass to me, and I headed over to say hello.

"Good speech, son," Dad said, waving me into a chair at his side.

"Are you and Clara . . ." Mom took a breath and wiped her eyes. "Are you back together?"

"Mom, are you crying?" I leaned in, a little worried.

"I can't help it. I'm just so proud of you both. I'm so happy."

"Son," Dad said, his voice taking the edge that told me he had something serious to say. I steeled myself and met his eyes. "I need to thank you. And to apologize."

"Oh."

"First, the fence. It looks great. And I think you know I needed your help because I just can't do that kind of thing myself anymore."

"Your heart," I said, trying not to be bitter that Dad still hadn't mentioned his health to me at all.

"Yeah. And I know that we handled that whole thing wrong. Your mom told me you were upset, and I didn't get it at first, but I think maybe I'm starting to. Because if it was you, I'd want to know."

"Right," I said.

"I don't think it's the same thing with parents," he said. "I never really got to know mine, so I think I didn't have the best example maybe. But if anything were to happen to you . . . well, Sly, you're my blood. And my first born. Dammit, you're my son . . ."

"I know," I said, hoping to maybe relieve my dad of the burden he seemed to be carrying. Clearly whatever gift for speeches I'd gotten had come from Mom.

"I'm trying to say . . . that I love you. That I'm proud of you. That you deserve to be treated like an adult."

I nodded, tears pressing at the backs of my eyes. Dad had never been emotional with me before. Never, not once. It was a lot to absorb. "I love you too, Dad. Thanks."

"Come home more often," he said, dropping my eyes and taking a swig of coffee.

"Okay," I said, chuckling. "I will."

"And Clara?" Mom asked, sensing that it was her turn to speak. She laid a hand on Dad's, and the silent gesture of support and love gave me a warm feeling inside.

"We'll see," I said. "We haven't made any promises. Things are complicated with work and Katie . . ."

"The things that matter aren't complicated," Dad said, still staring into his mug. "That's the lesson I've taken way too long to learn. Keep the people you love close. Trust them."

"I'll try," I told him.

Mom gave me a wide teary smile and on a breath she said, "Oh, Sly." It was almost sappy enough to send me into tears, so I stood and moved between my parents, dropping a hand on each of their shoulders and hugging them.

"I love you guys," I told them. "I'm gonna go see if Clara and Katie will dance with me."

Mom sobbed loudly, and I moved away, catching Clara's eyes as I headed back to the table where she and Katie sat. Even walking across the room toward her felt like coming home. It was that right.

Sure, there were complications to work out—how often would we be together, between our jobs and Katie's school? But I didn't care about any of that, because I thought Dad was right. The things that matter aren't complicated.

CHAPTER 28
CLARA

BIGFOOT IS ALWAYS A CONCERN

I'd driven to the lake with my heart in scattered pieces inside me. Now, as Sly prowled toward me across the crowded space of the reception party, I felt it pumping and strong—whole.

I loved him. There was no longer any reason to pretend it wasn't true. And hearing his words tonight had healed years of insecurity and doubt. Hearing him tell me he loved me too had stripped off all the layers of circumstance and difficulty that really came to nothing at all in the face of something as real as love.

"Would you ladies care to dance?" Sly asked Katie and me as he stopped next to where we sat, extending a hand in each of our directions.

Katie looked at Sly, and I could see the same love in her eyes that I felt for the towering man. But then she looked around and frowned. "It's a slow song, Silly. You can't dance to this."

"I bet your mom and I could," he told her.

"Let's try," I suggested, standing and taking his hand.

"I'm gonna sit with Miss Violet," Katie told us. "She looks sad."

I glanced over at Violet to see her holding a handkerchief to her face as Sam comforted her.

"Is your mom okay?" I asked Sly.

"She's overwhelmed with joy," he said. "Just not handling it well."

"Oh. Well, that's good, I guess."

Katie headed off to see Sly's parents, and I followed him out to the dance floor as "Wonderful Tonight" played around us.

Sly pulled me into his arms, and I breathed in the "dirty candy" scent of him I'd grown to love. It still set off tiny explosions of anticipation inside me. I pressed myself lightly against the solidity of his chest, resting my head on his shoulder as we swayed to the music.

There were other couples dancing under the soft lights with us, but as Sly held me in his arms, everything faded away except for us, together, in a perfect moment.

We didn't talk, not with words. But I felt myself telling him all the things I needed to say, and I felt every sentiment being returned in the soft touch of his hands, the steady beat of his heart.

When the evening wound down and people began to filter back to their cabins and rooms in the lodge, I knew we would have to say goodbye. Katie was here, and as much as I wanted to be alone with Sly, it wasn't going to happen.

"You sleepy, Katie bear?" I asked the exhausted little girl who'd gone back to the table and rested her head on it now, slumped forward in her sparkly green dress.

"Nooo," she moaned, her eyes shut.

I exchanged looks with Sly, who smiled at my daughter in a way that told me he loved her every bit as much as he loved me.

"What if I give you a ride?" Sly asked her.

One eye popped open as Katie seemed to evaluate his sincerity. "Okay." She reached out one arm, not lifting her head from the table.

"Not tired, huh?" I asked her.

"Just resting."

Sly scooped her up, and she wrapped herself around him,

dropping her head close to his as her arms locked around his neck.

I snapped a quick photo of them with my phone, wanting to remember this moment, when the big tough hockey player I loved held my daughter so tenderly—and her trust in him was clear in every relaxed muscle of her little body.

We said our goodbyes and headed out into the warm night. The sounds of the lake lapping the shore filtered through the air, along with murmurs from other partygoers and the occasional cry of a nightbird up in the towering pines overhead.

I took a deep happy breath and let it out, wrapping my arm through one of Sly's.

"Think there are any bears around?" he asked.

"Probably," I told him. "But they aren't interested in us."

"Bigfoot though," Katie supplied, her voice slurry with sleep.

"Oh right," Sly said.

I sighed. I'd have to tell Katie about Bigfoot in the morning.

We headed into the cabin I shared with my daughter, and took her into the smaller bedroom where a twin bed waited to receive her. She was asleep before Sly even managed to get her shoes off her feet. He placed a gentle kiss on her cheek and whispered good night to her, then turned to me.

"Should I see you in the morning then?" He blinked at me, shifting his weight.

"Or you could just wait a minute until I get Katie tucked in."

"I'll do that." He kissed my cheek softly and left the room.

After I'd tucked Katie in, thankful that she was soundly sleeping already, I stepped out into the tiny living space and pulled her door shut behind me.

There wasn't even time for a full breath before I was in Sly's arms again, his mouth finding mine.

My hands and mouth explored the once-familiar landscape of him again, as if rediscovering a favorite place. And I couldn't get enough.

I pulled him into the second bedroom and tugged his tie until he was stretched out above me on the bed, staring down at me in the dim moonlight coming in through the window.

"I missed you so much," he said. "God, I missed you."

"I missed you too," I told him, forcing my mind away from the tears I'd shed despite my promises to myself to be strong.

Sly undressed me slowly then, tenderly, following every touch to my skin with a soft kiss. He hung my dress over the back of a chair, and then I watched him with hungry eyes as he removed his tie, his shirt, and finally his pants.

We climbed beneath the light covers together, and as much as I wanted to jump him and remind myself exactly what his talented body could do to me, I took a long moment just to be. To appreciate that he was here. That we were together.

That he loved me.

And then I attacked him.

Sly's hands were everywhere, sliding across my skin as his mouth devastated my own, claiming me, pulling me closer and closer toward that glimmering edge of ecstasy.

I pushed his boxers from his hips, and felt him kicking them off beneath the covers, and then I traced a line down his stomach, loving the sharp gasp he made when I took him in my hand.

The soft velvet feel of him made me want him even more, and I didn't waste another second. I slid a leg over his hips and notched him right where I needed to feel him, welcoming him inside myself slowly.

Sly held me tightly as we joined together, his breath unsteady and his words low and dirty. "Fuck, you feel so good."

We were quiet and fast, each of us desperate for a release that reassured us of our connection, our solidarity. I came only a few moments after feeling him completely seated inside me, the satisfying fullness combined with the way he touched me and moved giving me little choice in the matter.

And Sly came moments after, stifling the roar I could feel in his chest by burying his mouth against my shoulder, his body tensing with each thrust before stilling with his release.

We lay in the darkness for what felt like hours afterward, pressed together, assuring ourselves this was real.

And when the first rays of sun fell across the bed, he was still there. I was still in his arms, and the joy that filled my heart was like nothing I thought I was capable of.

An hour later, after another sleepy roll together, the door popped open and a tousle-headed Katie stepped in.

"Did you guys have a sleepover?" she asked, climbing up onto the bed.

I froze, unsure how to handle this situation.

Sly was moving around as Katie climbed up the covers, and I realized he was pulling his boxers back on for her benefit. I reached an arm over to snag a big T-shirt out of the bag next to the bed and tugged it on.

"We did," I confirmed, sitting up a bit now that I had a shirt on.

"Did you sleep well?" Sly asked her as she nestled between us, her back against the headboard and her bear Tiddlekins in her arms.

"I think so. I don't remember going to sleep at all," she said, yawning. She looked between us. "Do you think there is a party again today?"

"No," I started to answer, but Sly interrupted me.

"There is, actually," he said, catching my eyes. "Family only. A brunch."

"Brunch?" Katie wrinkled her nose.

"Katie, we'll get some breakfast somewhere. Sly's family is going to spend some time together this morning."

"Aren't we Sly's family?" Katie asked. I swallowed my embarrassment at her presumption. She'd only voiced the very thing I wanted with my whole heart.

"Of course you are," he said. "And I would love to take you both to brunch with the rest of the family."

"You sure?" I asked him.

"I'm sure," he said. "And Katie, you better get ready."

"For what?" She tilted her little head up to meet his eyes.

"Well, one day soon I'm going to have to ask you a very important question."

"What's the question?"

"I'll ask you for your permission to ask your mother to marry me." Sly met my eyes over Katie's head briefly, and then looked back at Katie as my heart exploded inside me.

"Ask her now!"

"I think it's a little soon for that," he said. "But I'm going to ask her soon, okay? If it's okay with you."

"It's okay with me," she told him. "Maybe ask her tomorrow."

"Maybe," he confirmed.

My head was spinning as we got ready to go to brunch. Sly had to go back to his own cabin to get dressed, so we went with him. And as we walked up the stairs to the lodge for brunch, the word family played on repeat in my head.

Katie and I had lost so much—her dad, kind of, and then my parents all in the course of a year. I'd given up on the idea of her ever getting to have a real family. But now, here we were. And as we stepped into the space where Zara and Beck, Zara's parents, and Sly's parents all greeted us with enormous smiles and hugs, it felt an awful lot like coming home.

"I love you, Clara," Sly whispered in my ear.

"I love you too," I told him.

And soon, we were laughing together, surrounded by waffles and whipped cream, and the faces and hearts of the people I loved most in the world.

EPILOGUE - SLY

THREE MONTHS LATER

"Here you are again, always pushing the rules," Cade Simpson said, his arms cross over his chest and what I thought was a frown on his face beneath his enormous beard.

"She's not a puck bunny," I told him, gesturing toward the blonde at my side.

"She's also not a wife or a fiancée or a serious girlfriend." He winked at her, and my date for the evening giggled.

"Your beard is giant," she said, earning a squinty-eyed look from Cade.

"I like it this way," he told her.

"Can I touch it?"

He sighed and knelt on the concrete next to the pool in Mizzoni's backyard, and Katie reached out a tentative hand and touched his beard.

"It's soft," she said, sounding surprised.

"Of course it is," he agreed. "I take very good care of it."

"Like a pet," Katie suggested.

"Yep, that's Simpson's face weasel," I confirmed.

"Watch it," he said, shooting me a look.

"So can I stay? Even if I'm not a rabbit?" Katie asked him.

"I suppose. No trouble from you two though. Mizzoni's pretty sensitive after the foosball table got broken last time."

"I don't even like smoozeball," Katie assured him.

"Let's get a drink," I suggested to my tiny date, and the two of us took seats at the bar where Mizzoni waited.

"Hello Katie," he said politely.

"Hi Grumpy Goalie," she replied.

"Katie," I said, trying not to laugh. "Stephano is our host. Maybe we shouldn't call him names."

"You and Mommy call him that all the time."

"Lovely," Mizzoni said. "Also, probably fair."

"See?" Katie asked me.

"Is Clara coming soon? She has a civilizing effect on the two of you," he said, looking between me and my tiny sidekick.

"Mommy's coming later when she's done with work."

I'd been home a lot more lately, helping Mom with a few things, and taking up a bit of the slack for Clara so she could return to the field. Of course, time was short since the season was underway, but I took every chance I could get to see my girls. We had a bye this weekend, so Mizzoni had agreed to host. Things looked a little different during the season, however.

There were a few light beers around, but most of the guys didn't drink much during the season, so there were a lot more sodas and waters scattered across Mizzoni's outdoor space. There were radiant heaters blasting from above too, since the cold had come in hard and fast this year.

The feeling in our now-familiar gathering spot had gone from resort pool party to sedate cozy family gathering, and I had no problem bringing Katie around. These guys were my family, after all, and so was she.

Katie settled in at the table with Derek Reed, a new addition to the team who I still didn't know too well. He didn't talk much, mostly let his size and terrifying glare do the talking for him, but he and Katie had forged some kind of weird bond over jigsaw puzzles, and that's what they were focused on now. She probably knew Reed better than most of his teammates.

"Hey Clara!" Drea's voice caught my attention and I turned to see her hugging Clara, who'd just come around from the back gate. I slid off my stool and headed toward her, my heart beating out a happy rhythm that felt familiar now, since Clara had become part of my days and nights.

She and Drea exchanged a few words, smiling and laughing, and then I swept in, picking my girl up and spinning her around with a kiss.

"Hi," she said softly, her eyes meeting mine and sending my insides into the familiar melty shiver they did every single time she looked at me.

"Hey baby," I said, putting her back on her feet and kissing her cheek. "Get you a drink?"

"Sure," she said, taking my hand. I watched her eyes find Katie, assuring herself that her daughter was happy, and then she turned back to me. "How was your test?"

We settled back at the bar top, and Mizzoni leaned over to give Clara a kiss on the cheek and place a glass of white wine in front of her. "Was that today, Sly?" he asked.

Simpson, on Clara's other side leaned in. "Which one was this? Management Science?"

"Oh, dude. That sounds tough," Gillespie added, stepping close from behind us. "How do they test you on something they're calling a science that is seriously not a science at all? It's like they made some shit up and if you don't agree with all the pretend shit they invented, you fail."

I laughed, shaking my head. "It wasn't that bad. I don't think I aced it, but I think I'll pass."

"So how many more classes do you have, brother?" Simpson asked.

"Six," I told him.

"And then you're retiring for sure?" Gillespie asked.

Clara was beaming at me, the pride in her face so clear I

marveled at how it could possibly be directed at me. But it was. She'd told me that my life would be easier if I just told my teammates what I was doing. And she'd been right. I'd thought they would make fun of me, or maybe worry about me being distracted. But once again, I'd been shown I was wrong.

They believed in me. And they wanted me to succeed.

"Not for sure," I said. "But I want to have a fallback plan. I've been talking to Rhino more about the manager spot."

"Smart," Mizzoni said, nodding as his dark eyes found mine. "You'd be great."

Smart was a word I hadn't heard applied to me much, and the pride that washed through me at his praise was unfamiliar but not unwelcome.

Drea and Rock sat down next to Clara, and I watched as the woman I loved interacted with the rest of my favorite people in the world. Katie and Reed were giggling over in the corner, and the rest of the team laughed and talked beneath the warm glow of the heaters overhead. Light music wafted around us, and there was a sense of something I couldn't identify in the air. Something warm and close and comforting.

And when Clara turned and caught my eye, dropping a hand on my leg in a quiet check in to make sure I was doing okay, I realized that it was happiness. My life, since rediscovering the girl next door, was filled with happiness. And I wouldn't trade it for anything.

Want more of Sly and Clara's story? Get an exclusive bonus scene here: https://www.delanceystewart.com/wedding-winger-bonus

ALSO BY DELANCEY STEWART

Want more? Get early releases, sneak peeks and freebies! Join my mailing list here or scan the QR code and get a free story!

The Zamboni Diaries Series:

Checking the Center

The Wedding Winger

The Kasper Ridge Series:

Only a Summer

Only a Fling

Only a Crush

Only a Secret

Only a Touch

The Singletree Series:

Happily Ever His

Happily Ever Hers

Shaking the Sleigh

Second Chance Spring

Falling Into Forever

Singletree Box Set 1

Singletree Box Set 2

The Digital Dating Series (with Marika Ray):

Texting with the Enemy

While You Were Texting

Save the Last Text

How to Lose a Girl in 10 Texts

The Text Before Christmas

The MR. MATCH Series:

Prequel: Scoring a Soulmate

Book One: Scoring the Keeper's Sister

Book Two: Scoring a Fake Fiancée

Book Three: Scoring a Prince

Book Four: Scoring with the Boss

Book Five: Scoring a Holiday Match

Mr. Match: The Boxed Set

The KINGS GROVE Series:

When We Let Go

Open Your Eyes

When We Fall

Open Your Heart

Christmas in Kings Grove

The STARR RANCH WINERY Series:

Chasing a Starr

THE GIRLFRIENDS OF GOTHAM Series:

Men and Martinis

Highballs in the Hamptons

Cosmos and Commitment

The Girlfriends of Gotham Box Set

STANDALONES:

Let it Snow

Without Words

Without Promises

Mr. Big

Adagio

The PROHIBITED! Duet:

Prohibited!

The Glittering Life of Evie Mckenzie

9 781956 195156